'New Beginning'

A Novel

'New Beginning'

A Novel

Written By

Wilma Van Oort

iUniverse, Inc.
New York   Bloomington

A New Beginning

iUniverse books may be ordered through booksellers or by contacting:

iUniverse
1663 Liberty Drive
Bloomington, IN 47403
www.iuniverse.com
1-800-Authors (1-800-288-4677)

ISBN: 978-1-4401-2704-5 (pbk)
ISBN: 978-1-4401-2705-2 (ebk)

Printed in the United States of America

iUniverse rev. date: 4/29/2009

Dedication:

To my parents and siblings who have supported me in every way,
And to my good friend Emily who believed in my dream.

"Have mercy upon me, O Lord, for I am weak: O Lord, heal me: for my bones are vexed. My soul is also sore vexed: but thou, O Lord, how long? Let all mine enemies be ashamed and sore vexed: let them return and be ashamed suddenly."

Psalm 6: 2, 3 and 10

Chapter One

The preschool classroom at Elwood Elementary was full of loud and excited children running around with balloons and toys. It was the last day of Preschool for them and they were celebrating with a small party. Abigail Forrester stood off the side watching her twins, Cole and Chloe playing in the house area. Her son was most definitely a trickster, so she had to keep her eyes on him at all times. Last week he had brought worms in from the playground and put them in all the girls coat pockets. Screams were heard everywhere when they were leaving the classroom. He also loved hiding spiders in beds and in bubble baths, especially her own. However, who could resist his charming character and cute looks. Both Chloe and Cole looked alike, with brown curly hair, dark eyes and baby chub that was gradually thinning out.

"It certainly is too bad that Charles couldn't make it to the party, Abby. I know that Cole has been excited about today for weeks," Miss Tara, Abigail's friend and co-worker addressed, handing her a cup of punch.

Abby nodded and felt tears begin to form in her eyes, "Yes, he has just been so incredibly busy with work."

Tara took Abby's hand in hers, "I know what has been going on, honey. Chloe has been very forthcoming about his drinking. Has it been going on for a while now?"

"Yes, I've been trying to get him to stop, but that's only part of it, Tara. Charles has always been a very stubborn man but he became controlling and arrogant after the twins were born. We barely talk anymore and when we do

1

its about something I did wrong. He barely has time for the twins and when he is at home, he's sleeping on the couch or in his office."

"You should leave him and than maybe he will realize how badly he's been treating you all." Tara was a great friend but Abby did not like the fact that she knew about her marriage problems. She was the only one that could talk to her about normal things, and Abby never had to worry about the issues at home when they were together.

Over the years, she had gotten used to Charlie's controlling attitude and self-conceit, but the children never would. They barely knew him and he made no effort to join in on family life.

"Mrs. Forrester," a young student, Lila, exclaimed, poking her head around the door, "You're purse is ringing."

Abigail laughed and followed the blonde pigtailed girl over to the coat and shoes area. Sure enough, her cell phone was ringing and it was her husband.

"Hello, Charlie," she said softly, "Where are you?"

"Abby dear, I'm coming to you right now, I should be there soon. I've signed myself into the Greenwood Rehab Center and I want to take you and the twins for ice cream before I go in."

Abby's heart stopped for a second, she had waited so long for him to say those words. Now it didn't seem real. "Are you sure, Charlie? Can you do it?"

He sighed deeply, "I don't have a choice, Abs. For a long time now, I have been a terrible husband to you and I'm not a father to the children anymore. I want to change and I am going to prove it to you. Just let me come pick you up, I am already packed up and ready to move into the center."

Abby shut her eyes as tears began to flow down her face, "Oh Charlie, I have never been happier. We'll be waiting for you in the preschool classroom."

"That's great Abs, I'm sorry for everything."

"Don't worry about that right now, just get here okay?"

After hanging up, she let out all the tears she had been holding back. Everything was going to be all right. As the party thinned out, Abby told the twins their father was picking them up and watched them dance around in excitement. She knew exactly how they felt.

It didn't take very long for them to be bundled up and since the rain was coming down in sheets, they stood by the windows to wait. Tara came up to her, her purse in her hand and gave her friend a big hug, "Are sure you don't need me to stay?"

"Yes," Abby wiped away tears from her eyes, "I think we're going to be alright now."

"Alright, you've got my number if you need me." Tara waved goodbye to the twins as she left, but their faces were plastered against the window.

Abigail took out a mystery novel she had been reading and settled down for the wait. As time went by, she noticed the twins move back from the window and play on the carpet with farm animals. Soon she became so engrossed in her novel, that she didn't realize the time until Cole came and asked her. Almost an hour and a half had passed and he still had not arrived.

An unsettling feeling swept over her as she took out her cell phone and dialed her husband's number. When he did not answer by the fifth ring, she knew that something was wrong.

"Come on kiddos, I think Daddy forgot he was picking us up. Let's drive over to the Ice Cream Shoppe." Abby tried to keep a light tone in her voice, but by their long faces, she could tell they already knew.

They left the school and piled into her Bronco before heading onto the main road leading to the opposite side of town. As she drove, she could not help but feel nauseated, as if something terrible had happened. Her head began to pound and she could scarcely breathe, so she rolled down the window to get some fresh air. Glancing in the mirror, Abby groaned at the sight before her; her curly brown hair was slipping out of the braid and her eyes were puffy from crying. Charles would certainly have something to say about that.

"Mommy, look an ambulance and a fire truck," Cole exclaimed. At the sight of the bright flashing lights, Abby quickly pulled over the side and watched them hurry by. Breathing heavily in gasps, she looked back to the see the twins staring back with big eyes. Apparently, it had scared them as much as her. She carefully pulled back onto the road and sped up in order to see what had happened up ahead.

In the back seat, Cole and Chloe were singing 'The Bumblebee Song,' and Abby felt herself tense up before exclaiming, "No more singing please, Mommy has a headache."

As she was looking in the rearview mirror at the twins, she did not realize the standstill traffic up ahead. Chloe suddenly squealed and Abby slammed on the brakes for the second time.

"You were going fast, Mommy." Chloe said smartly, rubbing her eyes with the back of her hands.

Abby nodded, "Yes, Mommy was driving too fast. I'm sorry sweetie."

A police officer dressed in uniform came up to her window, "Good afternoon, Ma'am," he leaned down so he could see the twins in the back, "There is going to be a bit of a wait before the road clears up. There has been a bad accident on the other side of the overpass."

Panic seized within her, "Can...can you tell me what vehicle was in the accident?"

He rubbed his forehead nervously, "I believe a Black Jeep Cherokee, ma'am. They're bringing the male victim in now."

"NO! NO, it can't be!" she started to scream, as tears fell down her face, "Tell me it's not my husband."

The officer waved to his partner and together they helped her out and around the truck to the passenger seat. Than one officer who had been helping her from the start, climbed in beside her while the other took his place on the street. As they made their way to the other side of the overpass, Abby felt her heart pound louder and louder. The twins asked what was wrong but she did not know how to answer. The accident site was worse that she could ever have imagined. Charlie had driven right off the side of the overpass, through the railing and than landed down below up side down. An ambulance was just pulling away as they arrived and the officer pulled in right behind to follow them to the hospital.

"Where are we going, Mommy?" Cole asked, tears streaming down his face.

Abby turned back in her seat, "Daddy has been hurt, sweetie. We're going to the hospital so they can help him get better."

For the rest of the ride they drove in silence and once they arrived at the emergency entrance, Abby jumped out and helped the twins down from their seats. The officer took hold of Cole's hand and together they walked into the emergency. Abby prayed silently that he was all right, but when she saw the paramedics coming toward her she knew that he wasn't.

As they explained that he had died on the way to the hospital, she fell to the floor in sobs. Apparently, the wounds were too substantial and he had suffered major blood loss.

Over the next few days, family members continued to arrive with food and condolences. Abby could barely handle all the company but she was happy to see her mother come and take over. Cole and Chloe were nonexistent *throughout the week of Charlie's death. They spent their time in the attic, reading and talking together.*

On the third day, after the funeral services, Abby put the twins down for the night and settled down for some much-needed quiet time. She opened up an old scrapbook from high school and reflected back on the beginning of her relationship with Charles.

Back in High School, Abigail was a quiet and studious girl. Yet, she managed to catch the eye of the banker's son, Charlie Forrester. Charlie was warm, friendly, honest and a wonderful friend. And it wasn't too long after graduation that he proposed to her in front of both their parents. Although she had plans to go to college, she wiped that from her mind and said yes in a heartbeat. The wedding was a small event, and Abigail looked radiant. Everyone could see they were very much in love. Trouble roused in the family however, when Charlie received a proposal to work for a large corporate company in Allentown, which was not too far away. The hours were better and the pay more extravagant. Mr. Forrester, Charlie's father, was very angry since he expected Charlie to take over the family business when he retired. Although Charlie was saddened by his father's actions, he told Abigail he wanted what was best for them and she believed him.

A month later, they moved to the city, where Abigail also took up a job teaching at a local elementary school. The couple became very engrossed in their careers and rarely had time for each other. Abigail tried to pry Charlie away from the office for a few hours each week, but it was to no avail. He was trying hard to stay in his boss's top books. When Abigail heard the news that they were expecting, she hoped it would save their marriage. She did not believe in divorce, and she loved her husband hopelessly. Every day she prayed to God, asking Him to bring them together again. However, after the news of the pregnancy, Charlie became even more controlling. He demanded she quit her job and become a stay at home Mom. Abby didn't mind that, but she did mind her husband's manipulative habits. She could never do what she wished; her husband made every decision. When Abby went to buy paint for the baby room, he brought them back for a different color. Moreover, if Abby wanted to shop for baby clothes, he went along to the mall and chose everything himself. Abby got despondent, and very depressed; especially when her physician told her, they were expecting twins. And this was only because she had to go through everything for the second time; not because she didn't love the babies.

After the twins were born, Charlie named them Cole and Chloe.

Subsequent to the day, they were brought home and when Abby was alone with her mother; she told her all about her melancholy. When her mother asked if she still loved him, she immediately said that she did with all her heart. Her mother directly declared that just by knowing that everything would be okay. And she whispered that she would hint to Charlie about Abby's sadness at dinner.

That night, Charlie came home for dinner late, and Abby and her mother had already started without him. He was furious and called Abby into the kitchen where he threatened her that if she ate without him again she would be the one to go hungry. Abby knew that even though he said these things, he didn't really mean them; they had more than plenty of food in the house. Abby clung onto her faith and prayer and spent her days in the twin's room where all was quiet.

The following month, after that argument, things returned to normal. Charlie seemed to quiet down, and Abby was happy to be released of any judgment from her husband. Each weekend, Charlie would go out at night and would tell her he was going to a business meeting. Albeit she knew this was not true, Abby never asked him about it for she treasured the time alone with the twins. Chloe was a very bright child. Her dark curls and long eyelashes were enough to capture anyone's attention. Cole, on the other hand, was a loud and goofy child who continually teased his sister and played tricks on his mother. Charlie did not know these things however, because he rarely spent time with them.

A few years passed and the twins went to preschool. Abigail's life was much the same. She rarely saw Charlie, and when she did, it was to go to church or a business dinner, which acquired her company. Abby longed to teach again, and when she saw the advertisement at the preschool for supervisors, she jumped at the chance. Charlie was not too keen on the idea, however. He hollered at her, asking her why she couldn't be like his colleagues wives who spent their days at the spas and the malls. Abby was always a sensible girl, she did not like spending money on herself when other people in the world were starving and had nothing to their name. Since she couldn't get a job at the school, Abby decided she would spend the free hours of each day volunteering there. Her husband never had a clue, until one night after he had come home from a 'meeting' drunk. Cole innocently let it out at bedtime. He asked if Abby was going to finish a project they had been working on at school. Charlie started to think that Abby was no longer committed to him and he drank profusely. However, through all this, she loved him and never gave up on their marriage.

Tears flooded down her cheeks again, and Abby closed the scrapbook before her. Why had God taken him away just when he was going to get help? She knew that she could not ask this question because God did everything for a reason, but she felt so much pain. How would she survive as a single mother? Fatigue over came her racing thoughts and soon she fell asleep on the couch.

The leaves on the oak trees lining the opposite of the street were starting to change color, and Abigail Forrester sighed at its exuberance as she flipped the bookstore's sign to open, after her hour-long lunch break. So much had happened in this past year back in town, and it was starting to weigh down on her shoulders. Years before, Abby's Grandfather Daniel Richter had bought a little book store in the small town of Millersburg in the Pennsylvania County. Abigail would go with her mother to the store and help customers. She would also dream as she organized the bookshelves, of one day owning the store herself. Little did she know that one day her dream would come true.

Shortly after Charlie's funeral, Abby packed up their belongings and moved back to her hometown; the town she had forever missed. Now, with her grandfathers death just passed and the deed to a bookstore in her inventory; Abby felt like a completely different person.

"Cole Adrian Forrester, you leave your sister alone this minute!" Abigail scolded, from where she stood behind the counter of the "Bookworm." Her son, his brown eyes twinkling, had snatched his sister's book away from her and ran, asking her to scream and run after him.

Cole stopped in his tracks and smiled sheepishly, "Aww, Mom, I was just teasin'."

Abby raised her left eyebrow in question, "Oh yeah? Well, why don't you put your over-abundance of energy into some proper use; like dusting off the back book shelves?"

"Mom, I've got homework!" he replied, handing the book back to his sister.

Chloe giggled radiantly and announced, "We don't have homework Mommy. First graders never do, that's what Olivia said."

Olivia Bontrager, a young Amish girl happened to be Chloe's closest and most special friend. The twins went to an Amish only school, because the public elementary school in the small town had shut down due to a lack of teachers. Most of the children took a bus to a nearby town's school since the parents did not want anything to do with the Amish. But the Brothers had allowed a few children to come to their school, and Abby did not like the idea of her twins so far away each day.

"Why don't you both open the new boxes that arrived today? They're still in the back. You like doing that right?"

They cheered and ran to the back; Chloe's long curly dark hair bouncing as she went.

Abby smiled and shook her head; than took the price stamps and headed for the shelves to do inventory. It was roughly a half hour later; Abby was eating a cookie as she read a new novel behind the counter, when the clang of the metal chimes above the door rang and a tall, handsome Amish man walked in. Abby smiled and stood up, eager to greet a new customer.

"Good afternoon! Is there anything I can help you with?" She asked cheerfully, smoothing her hands down her skirt and shaking the cookie crumbs off that had reserved there.

He smiled, the dimple on his chin deepening, "Jah, in fact you can ma'am. I'm Olivia's Oom Levi. She told me I could find just about any book I wanted here."

Abby walked around the counter and stood in front of him, her blue eyes meeting his brown warm ones, "Well, she was right about that. What kind of book are you looking for?"

"I would like a book on carpentry. I started working for Frontline Construction in town, and I want to learn a little more than making furniture." He ran a hand through his dark curly hair.

Abby pointed to the back, "You've come to the right place, sir. We have a very wide selection. My Grandfather kept many because they are very popular around here."

Levi smiled, "Jah, I suppose so. Denki, ma'am."

"Anytime."

As he walked to the back, Abby noticed that something was different about him from that of the other Amish men she had met. She was still pondering over it when he returned later with a few books in his arms.

"I found some books that I think will help me out. You have a wonderful gut selection!" he announced, his brown eyes sparkling in excitement.

Abby smiled as she rang the books through the teller, "I'm glad you think so. We get new books in every month. I think it's good to have a wide selection."

Levi nodded and Abby than noticed what was so different about him; he didn't wear a beard. His face was clean-shaven and his hair was cut modernly as well. Yet, his manners, voice, and body language indicated that he came from the Amish origin.

"You can ask me, you know. I don't bite." He suddenly retorted softly, his face slightly flushed.

Blushing madly as she realized she had stopped what she had been doing to stare, she replied, "Ask what?"

He grinned, showing a set of perfectly white teeth; a gorgeous smile. "You can ask why I don't have a beard. I'm not scared to answer. That is what you were wondering, jah?"

Abby nodded shyly, "Yes, I did wonder about that. Your books come to $24.83."

As he handed her the money he spoke quietly, "I left the community when I met a girl at the age of nineteen. She passed away two years ago, so I came home. Although I am shunned, my brother allows me to visit."

"That must be awful; to not see your parents?"

Levi nodded, "Yes, it is. But I do not agree with the doctrine. When I met my late wife Sarah she told me all about her way of life, and about the God she had learned about."

"You're a Christian?" Abby asked quite surprised, "That's wonderful."

Grinning widely, Levi took his books off the counter and glanced around, "I believe I have seen you in church on Sundays. I sit upstairs so you wouldn't necessarily see me. Well, it was lovely to meet you Abigail. I hope we can meet and talk again sometime. Jah?"

"I'd like that," Abby responded quietly.

"Okay than; you have a wonderful gut day." He said over his shoulder as he retreated from the store.

Chapter Two

That night at dinner, Abby still could not stop thinking about that handsome man who had been so free to chat with her that afternoon. It would not have been unusual if he had only spoken out of politeness; but when he had spoken so openly she felt as if she had known him forever.

"Mommy, why are you staring at that wall so much?" Chloe asked; her mouth half full of spaghetti.

Abby sighed, "Chloe, please talk when your mouth isn't full of noodles. I'm just a little tired, sweetie," which was only the half truth.

"Me too." She replied smartly, "Mommy?" she again inquired, this time with her mouth empty.

Abby took a sip of her clear white wine before responding, "Yes, dear."

"Would it be okay if Olivia came over for dinner tomorrow? She said she never had a hotdog before. Isn't that weird?"

"Do you think her Mommy would say its okay? They are different than us you know; maybe she will not be allowed."

Chloe shrugged, "I dunno."

Cole, who until now had been reading a comic book at the table, than spoke up, "We're not allowed to visit with them, other than at school, Chloe.' Member what Brother Jesse said?"

Pouting profusely, Chloe nodded, and tears streamed down her cheeks, "Yes, I remember. He said that we could only come to the school if we did not play with the Amish children outside of class. Mommy, can you go ask her Mommy if its okay?"

"I don't see why not. But Olivia will have to come over another day than. Tomorrow is going to be too soon. Do you think you can wait?" Abby put a comforting arm around her shoulders.

Between sniffles, Chloe managed a yes and soon her tears disappeared.

After reading a passage from the Bible, Abby thanked God in prayer for their meal and the safety throughout the day. Than, with the twins help, she cleaned the kitchen and the dishes. They played Operation together until bedtime and than Abby got out Charlottes Web, their bedtime story.

Once their prayers had been said and they were both tucked into their beds, Abby sat beside Chloe. Her daughter asked softly, "Mommy, you won't forget to ask Olivia's Mommy will you?"

"No dear," Abby replied, kissing her on the forehead, "I won't forget. But, I can't promise you anything okay?"

Chloe nodded and snuggled in bed, "I love you one-hundred lollipops."

Smiling at their usual nighttime game, she replied, "I love you one-thousand red M&Ms."

The following morning, after the twins had gone to school, Abby started restocking the shelves with new arrivals. It was hard work. First she dragged the large boxes up front, than she sorted through each box, priced them all and lastly found the appropriate spot for them. Now the other books that had once vacated the shelves had to be arranged somewhere else; and so it kept going like a chain.

Just as she was dragging her last box to the front, the chimes rang and two Amish women stepped it. Each wore modest, dark blue dresses with long sleeves and a full skirt. The skirt held a lighter apron and a prayer covering was on their heads, secured around a tight bun.

"Good morning!" Abby greeted them, as she pushed a box behind the counter.

Both women smiled politely and called back the greeting in a Pennsylvania Dutch tone.

"Is there anything in particular you would like to find?"

The older of the two the woman, and the larger, stepped up to the counter, "We have not come for books, ma'am. We only have a question."

Abby smiled and nodded respectfully, "Okay, what is it you would like to ask?"

Again, the older woman smiled, this time more generously, "My name is Esther Stoltzfus, an' this is my sister Rebecca. We were wondering if you still have the back room empty. The sign you had up is off now, but we thought to inquire."

"It is still vacant, yes. I have a few boxes in it, but other than that its empty. What would you like to use it for, if I may ask?" Abby was very mesmerized by the idea of these woman using an Englisher's back storeroom.

Esther beamed at her composed sister in eagerness, "We need a larger place to hold our quilting bees, and also, we would like to have a place where customers can buy them."

"That's a brilliant idea." Abby enthused, smoothing down the wrinkles on her light flowered skirt. She stepped around the counter and held out her hand for them to shake, "My name is Abigail Forrester. Just come along with me and I'll show you the room. I hope it will suit you, I really loath having all this empty space."

It wasn't very long before the women headed home to collect their equipment so they could start. Abby was delighted to have the women in her store; it would be a wonderful change.

Later, after the morning rush had gone, Abigail sat down with a good book and a sandwich to have a break. It was quiet in the store and Abby suddenly felt very tired. A knock on the door a while later bolted Abby awake from where she slept on the table upfront. Embarrassed, she opened the front door where the Stoltzfus sister's stood patiently with two men behind them. Remembering her promise to Chloe, she asked Esther if she could keep an eye on the store while she did an errand. The woman assured her that everything would be fine and shooed her away.

As Abby drove her red Bronco through Lancaster's beautiful

countryside, she felt a sense of peace wash over her as she had never felt before. Looking at the directions she had received from a customer, Abby noted that she was almost at Olivia's home.

The street where the Bontrager's lived was typical of any other in Lancaster County. The road itself was straight and rolling. Between each home was a very long piece of street. As she pulled up to their home, she stopped to stare at its simplicity. The white washed two-story home was set between two large oaks bursting with autumn color. The long laneway drew up to the sheds and barns beyond the house. Abby continued once she got her bearings and caught sight of a very small boy in black pants, a white shirt, and black hat, run across the laneway from one of the sheds. He glanced nervously her way before disappearing from sight.

Abby parked her vehicle near the home and than walked towards the door. Just as she took a step up onto the patio, the door swung open and a small, pretty woman stood in the doorway. She was clothed in the same style of clothing as the Stoltzfus sisters.

"What can I do for you?" she asked bluntly, her hand on top of the little boy's head.

Smiling politely, Abby held out her hand in greeting, "My name is Abigail Forrester. Our daughters are friends at school."

Immediately the young woman smiled and gestured for her to come in, "Ach, come on in, jah? My name is Elizabeth, but you can call me Lizzie."

"It's nice to meet you. I hope I won't cause you any trouble by being here." Abby admitted amiably, as she took off her shoes.

Lizzie swung her hand as if waving her to stop, "Ach, don't worry. There is nothing wrong with meeting my daughter's favorite friend's mother, jah?"

They both giggled and than Lizzie asked if she'd like some tea. Abby agreed and sat down comfortably at the table, immediately liking this carefree, spirited woman. The young boy hid by his mother and peeked every so often at her curiously.

"What is your name, cutie?" Abby inquired, smiling at him.

When he didn't answer but turned away, Lizzie turned and replied for him. "This is little Abe. He is called after his Dat, jah? He's very shy, aren't you, Abe?"

Once the tea was steeped and on the table, the woman sat being acquainted; Abe came and sat down next to Abby, lightly touching the flowers on her skirt.

"The reason I came here Lizzie, was because of Chloe. She is very upset because Brother Jesse said that she could not have play dates with the children from your community."

Lizzie nodded, her eyes drifting shut for a moment, "I know, Olivia has been asking also. She says she wants to taste some of your different foods."

Abby smiled, running a hand through her hair, "Yes that is what Chloe told me."

"I cannot allow Olivia to go to your home Abigail. Although I wish I could for her sake, I cannot. My husband Abe would not allow it. His father is a Preacher as well and it would not look right for his granddaughter to be seen with an Englisher. I hope you'll understand." Lizzie explained, patting Abby's hand.

Sighing deeply, Abby nodded, "I'm trying, Lizzie. I really am; it's just so hard."

"I am glad you are trying. It is not easy for Englishers to understand the People; however it is not easy for us to understand you as well."

"Is there nothing we can do for them? Nothing at all?"

She shook her head, "No; not unless you cook here! Sometimes the Brothers will allow Englishers to stay for a few hours during the day."

Abby smiled, "Really? Or, are you trying to get a free meal from me?"

Laughing cheerfully, Lizzie shook her head, "Of course not. Ach, I love cooking for my family."

"I would love to cook a meal in your home, Lizzie. If you will let me," Abby decided, "I can cook something you have never had before, and the girls can play together also. Would that really be okay with the Brothers?"

Lizzie nodded, as she stood up and cleared away the dishes, "I think so. My husband will be busy on Saturday for a barn raising, but tomorrow will work. Is that too soon for you?"

Abby said it was perfect and than the two happily decided, that Lizzie would help cook the meal so she could learn. As Abby drove back home an hour later, she whistled to a melody from Brahms in her CD player. She was happy now that she had made a new friend.

The following day, Abby made a decision with Esther Stoltzfus that she would work in the store when Abby couldn't as payment for the use of the back room. Mrs. Stoltzfus was very happy with the arrangement and it couldn't have worked out better for Abby.

After lunch, Abby headed to the Super Market for the ingredients she needed. The menu she had decided on was lasagna, garlic toast, Caesar salad with lemon pie for dessert. The latter had already been made the night before, so only the meal needed to be prepared. An hour later, Abby knocked on the Bontragers back door, her arms loaded with groceries.

Young Abe opened the door, "Hello," he greeted, his smile showing missing front teeth.

"Hello, Abe. Can you help me carry the groceries inside?" Abby asked, as she tried to slip inside before the screen door slammed shut.

A deep familiar voice answered her instead of Abe's quiet one however, "There's no need, Abe. I can help Ms. Forrester; you run along and collect the eggs."

Abby looked up into the twinkling eyes of Levi, the handsome man who had so captured her thoughts the previous day.

"Hello Levi." Abby said breathlessly, as he took a few bags out of her hands, "I didn't know you'd be here."

"I always eat dinner here on Friday nights; did not Lizzie tell you?" he replied nonchalantly.

"No, I believe she declined on mentioning that. That's alright though, I have plenty of food."

Levi nodded as his gaze slid over the groceries on the table, "I see that. Are there any more in your car?"

"Just some wine, I believe."

"We should save that for later, jah? The People do not drink, Abigail. Perhaps I can have a glass with you later?" he winked at her, and smiled as her cheeks turned red.

Lizzie joined them a little while later and Abby showed the first few steps to her so they could start. While they were busy cooking dinner, Levi took the horse and buggy to pick up the children. Abby smiled when he left, knowing how excited the twins be to ride in it.

"Levi seems like a wonderful man." Abby said, as she stirred the tomato sauce.

Chuckling softly from where she sat at the table chopping veggies, Lizzie agreed readily, "Jah, he is a good man. Abe and Levi are very close brothers; and they would do anything for each other."

Abby turned the gas element lower and than sat across from Lizzie. "Do you get in any trouble with having Levi around?"

"Not anymore. Abe's father came by consistently at first with the other Brothers. My husband told them that the Bible spoke of loving our neighbors. He said that if they were told not to then there was no point in believing in the Amish way of life." Lizzie leaned forward as she spoke, as if telling a secret.

"Wow." Abby proclaimed, "That must have been hard."

Nodding silently, Lizzie went back to making the salad and cutting veggies, "They still don't agree with us, but Abe is persistent to stay friends with Levi. Yet, the Brothers do not think it is right not to follow the shunning. A bad seed may corrupt others; they say. But, Levi really needs us; he has been through so much in the past."

The pan which held the long and wide noodles started to boil over and Abby jumped up to take care of it as she spoke, "I heard what happened to Sarah; he told me the other day in the store."

"He told you what happened? That is strange." Lizzie frowned, her pretty face wrinkling up a little as she pondered.

Abby blushed and hid her face, "Well, I noticed he didn't have a beard. He caught me staring."

Lizzie laughed gleefully, "I'm sure he had fun watching you blush, jah? Our Levi is a tease; that is for sure."

The back door slammed shut suddenly and the women looked up. Abe Bontrager stepped into the doorway and gazed at the Englisher in his kitchen laughing with his wife. He wore broad fall trousers, suspenders and a dark blue shirt. A beard framed his face, but there was no mustache above his lip. His eyes were what struck Abby though, they were penetrating and intriguing.

"Abe, this is Abigail Forrester. She is cooking us a wonderful gut dinner tonight." Lizzie announced, as she went to greet her husband.

He nodded solemnly, "Nice to meet you Ms. Forrester. I do not mind you cooking, just as long as my stomach gets filled."

Abby smiled at this quiet and withdrawn man, "I hope you enjoy the food too, sir. We are doing our best to give you a treat."

At that, Abe's eyes twinkled, "I am sure I will be satisfied, jah?"

Lizzie patted her husband's stomach, "Jah, you always are dear."

Abby hid her smile behind her hand and than lifted a large noodle out of the pan and threw it against the wall.

Abe gasped, "What are you doing with the food?"

Shaking her head in exasperation, Lizzie spoke up, "You will not have to eat that, Abe," than she looked at Abby in question, "jah?"

"Jah." Abby said, trying to sound like them, "I'm just checking if they are ready. If the noodle sticks to the wall, they are ready. Since it's still stuck, I assume they are."

It wasn't long before Levi came into the kitchen with the children trailing behind him. The food was not out of the oven yet, so they sat down talking in the living room. Once the cheese on the lasagna was melted, they went about setting the tables. Abe had set up a smaller table for the children, to make more room for the adults. Levi took the dishes steaming with food to the table and than sat across from Abby. Once everyone was sitting down, Abe started prayer.

After dinner, Chloe and Olivia helped their mothers' clean up the dishes. Levi left for a while and than came back when the dishes were finished.

"Are you ready for that glass of wine?" he asked, leaning against the doorframe.

Abby wiped her soapy hands dry and than nodded. They took their glasses of wine out to the gazebo swing and sat side by side, swaying slowly. Levi glanced at her from time to time, but said not a word.

Abby interrupted the nervous silence after a long while, "Is construction the career you want?"

"Actually, I am studying for six years now to be a doctor, and I have only about a year to go." Levi announced staring down at his glass.

Abby smiled up at him, "That's really great. You would make a wonderful doctor."

Turning his bronzed face toward her, he raised his eyebrows in question, "Do you really think so?"

"Yes," Abby proclaimed, "You are very nice, easy going and very patient and good with children. I think you would be great."

Grinning widely, he patted her hand lightly, "Denki. I cannot believe you have learned all that by knowing me so short a time."

"I have to know how to read people when I work in my bookstore. That way I can find out what each customer likes to read."

"Ach, I see now what you mean," he stood up for a moment and refilled their glasses, before rejoining her on the bench swing.

Abby stared at her glass, "It has been a very long time since I shared a glass of wine with a man."

Levi nodded and continued to push the swing back and forth, "It is the same for me."

"I am very happy now. My children are doing well in school; they have made new friends very quickly. Yet, I feel like I am missing something in my life!" Abby reflected quietly.

"How long has it been since your husband passed, Abigail?" Levi inquired.

"A year and a half, yet it seems like much longer. Charlie wasn't what I first thought he was. Although I loved him, our marriage was very difficult."

Levi shook his head, "That is too bad, jah? Sarah and I were very happy together, but she could not have children. My father said that it was punishment for leaving the People."

"Surely you do not believe that! God brought you two together for a reason."

"I now know that it was to follow Him." He smiled down at her and than stood up, "It's getting late and I'm sure your little ones need rest. Shall we say good night?"

Abby took his outstretched hand and allowed him to pull her up. Meanwhile she contemplated the formality and decency that surged from him. Together they walked back the house to say farewell. Chloe was playing with some dolls in the corner and Cole sat with Abe who was telling him a story. Smiling at the tranquility about her, she went against her will and disturbed the peace.

Chapter Three

Monday turned out to be a scorcher, and Levi was working hard putting shingles on the roof of an elderly woman's home. The work was hard to do single handedly, but he really enjoyed it. On his breaks, he took out his books and studied, so far he was exceeding in his expectations and hoped he could keep up the marks.

Just as he was climbing down the ladder for lunch, his cell phone started to ring. Muttering to himself about never getting used to it, he jerked it out of its pouch.

"Levi here." He greeted abruptly.

Todd Landers, his boss and friend was on the other end, "Hey Levi, is everything going okay over there? Or do I need to send someone to help."

Levi wiped the sweat from his brow with a handkerchief and than open his water jug, "Everything is fine here right now, boss. I should be done in an hour or so."

"Great. You have class at three, right?"

"Jah, that's right."

Todd sighed heavily, "When your class is over, do you think you can help pour for a while? We're starting pouring the concrete by the new church and we could really use your help with the finishing."

"I'll be there. Say around 9:30?"

"Thanks buddy." Todd said with obvious relief, "That's great; you deserve a raise with all the extra hours you have been putting in."

Levi laughed, "Jah? That is wonderful gut. Denki, boss."

"Alright than, I'll see you later, Levi."

"Bye boss."

After putting his cell back in its pouch on his hip, he sat under the front oak tree that spread nearly over the entire lawn to eat under its shade. He was exhausted but happy. With his new raise, he could cut back on all the hours he was working to pay off his student loans.

Levi was putting his lunch box back in the truck when the elderly woman who owned the house came up to him.

"Hello dear," she greeted warmly. Her grey hair was turned up in a roll on the back of her head, and she wore a long summer dress and a wide smile upon her face.

"Gut day." Levi responded friendly as he closed the truck door behind him.

"I made some fresh cinnamon buns and I was wondering if you'd be interested in one."

"Denki, Mrs. Richter. That would be wonderful gut." Levi's mouth watered already, just by imagining the treat.

Levi followed Mrs. Richter inside and sat down at the kitchen table where she indicated.

"So, how long have you been gone from the Ordnung, Levi?" Rose Richter inquired bluntly after joining him at the table with the buns.

"How do you know about the Ordnung, ma'am? Many people do not know about this; unless they are acquainted with the Amish." The woman who seemed to see right through his barriers surprised Levi.

"I've known a man from the People. We were in love but in the end, he chose a woman from the church. It wouldn't have worked anyway; he was very attached to the plain life." Rose explained as she sipped her coffee, "But I can see you have left. Was it hard dear?"

Levi found the tightness around his heart lessoning around this warm-hearted woman, "Jah, it was."

"Do you still see your family?"

"Not my Mamma and Dat, but my brother, Abe I see. Every

Friday I eat dinner at their home." Levi finished the bun in between speaking and than leaned back in his seat to drink the coffee before him.

Rose nodded, "Yes that must be nice to at least see them. I think that's the reason Abram stayed behind, he couldn't bear to lose his family."

Levi straightened, "Abram? What was his last name, if I may ask?"

"Bontrager," she responded, "Why do you ask?"

Paling in the face, his eyes showed disbelief, "That is my father, Mrs. Richter."

She held a hand to her heart, "Oh dear, I've certainly made a mess of things haven't I?"

Lifting his hand to stop her distress he said, "No, not at all. If anything, you have made me understand my Dat better!"

"Is he such a difficult man still?"

Levi laughed, "Jah. I haven't seen him in a few years, but my brother tells me he is still stubborn."

Rose smiled and stood up to clear away the dishes, "Your father was always a difficult man to understand. But underneath that big web he wound around himself, he was a charming, intelligent, and caring person. What is your mother like; Catherine, right?"

"Jah, she is a very wonderful woman and mother. She took care of us so gut. She wanted to have a large family, but she was diagnosed with endometriosis after I was born. Yet, she always said that God gave us both to her as a special gift. Around Dat she is always a different person; giddy, happy and compassionate."

Rose wiped the coffee stained counter till it shone as she spoke, "Your mother sounds like an amazing person."

Levi stood up to get back to work, but stopped at the door, "Denki for the treats, ma'am. And may I be frank?"

"Of course, dear."

"Did you remarry after my father left you?"

Rose went to the china cabinet next to the front door and showed him a picture of a man in a sailing outfit out on a lake. "Dan and I were married for forty years. He passed a half a year ago from cancer, but he fought it hard."

Levi smiled at Rose and saw the love for this man still in her eyes, "That's gut that you had someone."

After his class that night, although he was extremely tired, Levi headed over to the church foundation. A few other men, along with Todd, were still working and Levi immediately started smoothing the concrete down with a trowel. As he worked, he thought about the tiny woman who had loved his father so entirely. When he had finished the roof, Rose had asked him to come back. She had pictures she wanted to show him. Levi immediately agreed, he wanted to get to know her.

It was nearly midnight when the work was finished, and as Levi was cleaning his tools a couple of the other men came up to him.

"Hey Levi, we're going for a drink at Grey's Pub; want to come?"

Levi shook his head, "No denki. I do not enjoy pubs, and I only drink occasionally."

They shrugged, "Alright than, see you later."

After they tore off together in one truck, Levi spent nearly an hour cleaning up around the site. Once he was satisfied it was organized he headed home.

"Hey Levi, how's your paper for Biology coming?" a voice interrogated from beside him in his late afternoon class the next day.

"Gut. I am writing each night for a little while." Levi responded cheerfully as he put his books in his briefcase. The man who sat beside him was a red haired, freckle faced, brilliant student, who loved helping others. Levi was very appreciative to have him sitting near.

Pete Schites smiled, showing a row of braces, "That's a good idea. I do the same, but in the morning. At night I can't stay awake very long."

Levi chuckled and followed his classmate out into the hallway; "I guess everybody functions differently throughout the day."

"Hmm," Pete murmured, "Listen, I'm sitting in at an investigation on a body at the coroners this evening. He's a friend of mine; would you like to join me?"

Levi shuddered, "Denki, but I'd rather work on living people. I know there need to be people to confirm death, but I am not the person."

Pete slapped him good-naturedly on the shoulder, "I hear you. Well, see you tomorrow than."

As he drove home after stopping for a bite to eat, Levi contemplated his friend's invitation. It would have been interesting to see the human organs up close without other students in his way. Deciding he'd rather go than be home alone, he turned his truck around and headed to the morgue.

"Hey you came?" Pete announced at the door; he wore gloves, a gown and goggles, making him look very strange.

Levi walked past him into the cold room. A tiny man dressed just like Pete said a curt greeting and than continue working on the body.

"Scrub up Levi; and than dress up. We're just about ready to start."

The evening proved to be very productive and interesting. It wasn't long before he started to loosen up and take notes. Later as they all scrubbed up again, Levi thanked Pete for the opportunity, for he now had more material for his final paper.

It rained the next day, and Levi didn't have to work. He slept in and than started sorting through all his note cards. As he was busy, the phone rang and Levi ran into the kitchen to pick it up.

"Hello."

A soft familiar voice spoke on the other end, "Is this Levi?"

Levi smiled, "Yes, this is."

"It's Abby from the Bookworm. I just wanted to let you know that we got a new shipment in and there are some books on health and also some on construction."

"Oh, denki for calling; Abby. I'll come by this afternoon before my evening class. I'm doing some homework right now, but I'll stop by after lunch than."

She sighed as if in relief, "Great, I'll see you than."

After he hung up, Levi wondered what that sigh had meant. Did she want to see him again? Or did she just want to sell some more books? Levi worked for another hour and than opened his fridge to see what he could eat. A large bowl of Waldorf salad from Lizzie sat enticingly in his vision. He made a sandwich and than took the salad bowl to the table. After praying, he dug in; happy to be saving money by not eating out again.

Chapter Four

Shaking the drops of rain off his insulated bomber jacket, Levi looked around the store, until he saw Abby, her dark curly hair gleaming and her striking eyes radiant. His heart leapt in his chest; she was a vision.

"You came," she said softly, coming up around the counter.

Levi shook out of his coat and folded it over his arm, "I said I would."

She blushed prettily, "Yes, you did."

"How have you been?" Levi asked warmly.

"Good; and you?" she replied courteously, a slight blush spreading over her face.

Levi grinned at their small talk, "I've been gut. You would never guess what I saw last night without any students pushing and shoving."

Abby pointed to the table at the front of the store, "Well, sit down and tell me all about it."

"Yesterday, a friend of mine from college, asked me to join him and visit a friend of his. His friend is a mortician and he was investigating a body."

Abby's eyes widened in surprise, "Wow."

Levi beamed, his eyes shining brightly, "Jah, I know. At first, I did not want to go, but I was so curious to see. So, I turned around on my way home and went. It was amazing. There was no one to take over from me, and I could just take my time."

"I can't imagine seeing that. It would scare me to bits. I'm not very good around blood."

"I think that all changes when you are learning about the human body; you look at things differently." Levi explained, folding his arms on the table; "When I was young, Dat would let me watch when he butchered a pig or the chickens, and I almost always fainted. Now, I don't feel light headed at all."

Sighing, Abby nodded in agreement, "I guess that makes sense. My brother Mike is in the Marine Corps right now. He used to always hurt himself; at least once a day. And every time I would have to leave the room while my mother patched him up."

Levi laughed, "We're two peas in a pod, jah? If only I would concentrate more on the organs than the blood."

"You said you will be finished in a year right? How does it feel to be almost done?"

"Very gut. I will be doing practicum at the local hospital this year, so in about two weeks I'll be stopping at Frontline."

Just as he was finishing his last sentence, the metallic sound of the tinkling door chimes interrupted their conversation. Abby excused herself to help the customers. Levi watched the emotions flash across her face as she spoke to them; from happiness, to concern and than to sadness. Tears welled in her eyes, and Levi felt like embracing her. Abby continued to talk to the elderly woman and her friend; so Levi walked around the store and looked for the new books that had come in. After the customers had left, he went up to the counter with two books; both from Grey's Anatomy.

"Are you alright, Abigail? It looked like you received bad news." Levi asked softly, as he watched her dry the tears from her eyes.

Abby nodded, "I think I'll be okay now. The woman, who just came in, was a friend of my grandma. We know each other very well; she is like a grandmother to me. She just told me she has a brain tumor."

"Ach," Levi went around the counter and took her into his arms. She tensed up at first, but he just rubbed his hand over her back calmly, "I'm so sorry your friend is sick, Abby."

Abby suddenly let loose and started to sob, clinging to Levi for strength. When finally her sobs turned to sniffles, she whispered, "Can you take me to my mothers, Levi?"

"What about the twins? They come home from school soon, jah?"

Abby leaned back to look in his face, her eyes were all puffy, "They're spending the day with Charlie's parents."

Levi patted her comfortingly, "Alright than, let's go."

They closed up the store and than left to her mothers. She gave him directions as to where to go; he laughed when he realized where they ended up, it was Rose Richter's house.

"What's so funny?" Abby asked curiously, as she unlocked the seatbelt.

"I just redid your mother's roof. She invited me in for coffee and we had quite a visit."

Abby smiled, "Really? That's a coincidence, hey?"

Rose was just as surprised as Levi had been. She immediately set about preparing tea, and told them to take a seat in the living room. Her living room was beautifully designed in blues and yellows. A white fireplace took place in the center, with a mantle filled with pictures above.

"This is very nice. In my home where I grew up, we had no colors. Now, I cannot get enough color in my life."

Abby sat down on the couch, tucking her feet under her, "Was it very hard to get used to life after you left?"

Levi turned to her and sat down beside her on the couch, "Jah, it was very hard. I find life is very fast now, compared to the Plain life. It is not as peaceful, that's for sure."

"I think we just have to find peace for ourselves. A hobby, relaxation, exercises; all these things can contribute to peace. It's just a different kind."

Together they sat chatting while Rose puttered around in the kitchen getting tea and biscuits ready. The house and the company she held were comforting; it was easy to feel like himself around her. Abby sat very comfortably on the coach. She had pulled a small afghan from the chair beside her and wrapped it around her legs to ward off the sudden chill that swept through the room. Her long curly hair, so much like her daughters, framed her face softly making her look very vulnerable and almost childlike.

"Well, kiddos. What brings you here today?" Rose asked as she swept into the room with a tray in her arms. She placed it on the coffee table and went about serving them both.

Abby told her mother in a quiet tone all about Violet's visit to the store. Rose than sat down in a recliner and frowned, "Why did she go to you and not me? She comes by so often, and she's never told me a thing; that stubborn woman!"

Smiling at her mother's complaint, Abby leaned forward, "I know she is stubborn, Mom; but maybe she realized that she had to tell someone and did not know how you'd react."

"I'm sure she is very upset by what is happening. Having a brain tumor is very serious. It is not always a good idea to operate because so much could be lost at the twitch of the physician's hand." Levi explained stirring sugar into his cup of tea.

Rose just shook her head, "I cannot believe it; I went through all this already with your father, Abigail. I don't think I have the strength anymore."

"Mom we will just have to pray that God will give us the strength to help Violet through this."

Levi felt out of place for he did not know Violet, and he stood up unsure of what to do.

Clapping her hands together, Rose stood up also and pasted a bright smile on her face, "Well, lets not get sad now when we know not what will happen; lets do something fun." Rose walked to the china cabinet and bent onto her knees in front of it as she muttered, "It should be under here somewhere."

"What are you looking for Mom?" Abby asked innocently, "Did you lose your reading glasses again?"

Rose said nothing and than spoke again to herself happily, "Aha, I knew you were under here."

When she stood up, she held a small box in her hand, which she than held out to Levi, "Open it, dear!"

Levi obliged and found himself staring into his father's eyes. Only this man was unlike any father he knew. Instead of the circle cut hairdo he now wore, this man's hair was short and spiky. Since he was not married when the photo was taken, he also wore no beard. His hand held a sweater over his shoulder and a wide smile was on his face.

"He looks so different." Levi exclaimed, as he sat down on the coach again.

Rose laughed and than urged him to keep looking. Levi searched through the box, finding more pictures of his father and Rose together, a notebook, a sketchbook full, or drawings of a younger Rose and a handcrafted cigar box.

Abby looked at her Mom in disbelief, "You dated Levi's father?"

"Yes, Abram is Levi's father. We just found out the other day; isn't that something?" Rose's eyes glittered with amazement, as if she had never heard of anything like it.

"May I ask why you kept this old cigar box?" Levi asked, holding it up into the light to look it over more closely.

"Your father left it here the day he left; I loved the smell of his cigars." Rose said, her eyes clearly lost in a stream of memories.

Levi open it and took out a long packaged cigar, "My Dat always told me not to smoke or chew; he said it killed your lungs. He never told me he had smoked in his Romspringe."

"Levi," Rose asked softly, "Will you give that box to your father? I think its time I let go of it; he will want it back. He made it himself; isn't it beautiful?"

Levi nodded truthfully as he closed the box again and than stood up, "Ladies, I have to get going. My class starts at 7:30 this evening and I must prepare my notes and do some reading yet."

Abby stood up and walked with him to the door where she stopped him by holding onto his arm, "Wait, Levi. I want to thank you for being here when I needed someone. That was very sweet of you."

"That was no problem, jah? I quite enjoyed your company, Abigail." Levi patted her hand gently and than shrugged into his coat, "You will be okay than?"

"Yes, I will be okay. Have a good class; and don't study too hard."

Laughing softly, Levi walked out to his truck and backed out the driveway. When he looked in his rearview mirror later, he saw her still standing on the porch with both arms folded around her.

The class that night was all about preparing for practicum. As Levi sat in one of the upper seats in the room, his mind continually wandered to the sweet and caring woman, he was beginning to know. The professor droned on and on, and the assistant started handing out booklets about practicum to all the students. This would be his second practicum so he already knew what would take place. He would work alongside a doctor and assist in many cases. Hopefully he would get to do more than just assist this time. On his last practicum, the doctor rarely let him do anything, except finishing up after the he left.

"Alright students, we will now have a pop quiz, get ready to call out the answer when I say your name." The professor suddenly exclaimed from the podium.

Levi groaned out loud and Pete gave him thumbs up sign. More than once, Levi had blanked out when he had just known the answer. The pop quizzes worked by pictures flashing across the screen; when it stopped at a certain picture the professor would call out a name and the student would have to answer immediately. These pictures included diagrams of organs, nerves and arteries, and others were of diseases and broken bones.

This time, when Levi's name was called, he was prepared and as he rambled off the answer, Pete shook his head. Pete also said an answer, but in the end, Levi was right. He grinned at Pete and gave him the thumbs up sign. Pete just shook his head remorsefully.

After class, they went to a corner café to have a drink and talk. Pete told him he already received a proposal to work in Meadowland Hospital, the main facility in the town. Levi was hardly surprised by this, since he had seen the brilliance and efficiency, which came from the man's hands.

"What about you Levi, have you received any propositions yet?" Pete asked, taking a big bite from his cherry pie.

Levi shook his head, "No, but I'm thinking of doing some mission work after we graduate."

Pete looked up amazed, "Really? You don't get paid very well for that, you know? My cousin does mission work, and she hardly makes enough to live on."

"I know. But that is not the point; I wish to help those in need and I don't really have far to go." Levi explained as he ate his brownie and whipped cream.

"No; I guess not. What about your old church community? Don't they need doctors?"

Shaking his head, Levi's eyes blazed a little, "They are a stubborn people, Pete. If I would stay in the community, I would be going against my own beliefs even though they need more physicians."

"I see what you are getting at. They will think that you intend to bring everyone to your belief!"

"Jah that is right, Pete."

They sat in silence until Levi professed that he was very tired and that he had to work the next day.

The week passed by uneventfully; as Levi was very busy with work and school. Todd had asked him to work part time if needed during his practicum. Levi said he couldn't promise him anything, but he would love to help.

By the time Sunday arrived, Levi was so exhausted he had to push himself to get ready. He arrived just as the bells were ringing to announce the start of the service. As Levi slid into his pew, he searched the bottom floor for Abby and her twins. He found the twins sitting with Rose, but Abby was nowhere in sight. Worried, he prayed along with the minister but found his mind wandering. When he sat back down after prayer, the organ began to play softly and somehow it sounded different from usual. That was when he found her; she was on the organ. Her long dark hair flowed down her back; and her fingers flew across the keyboard with grace. Obviously, the organist was sick or otherwise with-held and she was taking her place.

Once the benediction had been said, Levi went outside and waited for Abby who would continue to play until everyone had vacated the church. He leaned against the side front of the building, and crossed his feet at the ankles holding his face up to the sun.

"Levi, is that you?" a cheerful familiar voice asked, breaking him from his thoughts. Levi looked down into the bright eyes of Rose Richter.

"Gut day, Mrs. Richter." He greeted warmly, happy to be in her company.

Rose laughed, "Oh, please call me Rose, dear. How have you been? Is school going okay?"

Levi smiled and obliged her by telling her about his upcoming practicum. Suddenly however, Rose's face paled, "Oh dear," she muttered.

Following her gaze, he noted Abby talking to an older couple who seemed to be very worked up about something.

"Stay here Rose. I'll see what I can do!" He said sternly, noticing Abby's drooping in exhaustion.

Levi walked up to Abby and called out, "Abby is that you?"

Abby turned, a sign of gratitude in her eyes, "Levi," she greeted softly.

"You'll have to excuse me, but I just had to see you. Sorry to interrupt."

"Oh, it's quite alright," she replied hastily, "Have you met my in-laws Roger and Gwen Forrester?"

Levi shook each of their hands and than excused them, pulling Abby with him gently. Abby's eyes were filled with tears and she was shaking terribly. Not wanting to pry into her personal life, he just took her to her car and than Rose came up with the twins and said, she would drive Abby home. They had driven together anyway, so it made the most sense; however, Levi felt left out.

At home an hour later, he heated up a can of tomato soup and made a sandwich for lunch. As he ate, he thought about the despair he had noted on Abby's face when he had walked up. He wanted desperately to go and see her, but Sunday's were not the best time to visit. All afternoon he sat with a book open on his lap and his mind dwelling on Abby. After dinner, he gave up trying to stay away and headed to Abby's apartment

The lights were all on when he pulled up in front of the store. He knocked three times on the side door leading up to their home. Light footsteps ran to the door, when it opened he found Chloe before him dressed in a pink nightgown.

"Mr. Levi, why are you here?" she asked bluntly from the other side of the screen.

Levi smiled, "I came to see how your Mom is doing."

Chloe opened the screen door, "She's really sad today. She cried all afternoon; Grandma stayed for a while, but she went to visit someone in the hospital."

"Where is your Mom now?"

"She's in the living room; she was just reading to us about King David when you came." Chloe exclaimed, pulling him down the hallway after he had kicked off his loafers.

Abby sat on the coach with her arm around Cole who was leaning onto her. A thick blanket covered them and Chloe ran over and snuggled down under on the other side of her Mother.

"Hello Levi," she said with a small smile, "What brings you here?"

Levi blushed, "I came to see how you are doing. You seemed fairly upset, jah?"

"Yes, I am. I'll tell you about it later when the twins are in bed."

"I'll go make us some coffee while you finish reading to the twins."

In the kitchen, Levi found a can of decaf coffee grounds and set about preparing the drink. He opened the fridge once the coffee was percolating and found a strawberry-rhubarb pie on the top shelf. He put the oven on and placed the pie in it. Warm pie and ice cream sounded like the perfect ending to the evening. The twins ran into the kitchen a few minutes later as he was pouring the ready-made coffee into two mugs.

"Mr. Levi, we have to say good night," Cole exclaimed, rubbing his eyes with the back of his hand, clearly very tired.

Levi gave them both a generous hug and a gentle kiss on the forehead. Abby watched from the doorway, her hair slightly mussed and her dress wrinkled. Levi had never seen a more beautiful sight than what was before him now.

While Abby left to tuck the twins into bed, Levi brought the pie and coffee to the living room. He had just settled back on the coach when she walked in the room rubbing her eyes as she yawned, than took a seat beside him.

"You made pie." She said in amazement.

He grinned, "No, you did. I just warmed it."

That brought a smile from her lips, "Yes, I did. Yesterday Chloe wanted to bake a pie, so we made four. You can take one home, the rest are in the freezer."

"Denki; I will enjoy some home baking. I'm afraid I'm not the best cook." He admitted between bites.

Abby snuggled back under the blanket and than put the plate on her lap as she ate, her dark curls falling over her shoulder.

"I never knew you could play organ." Levi than said, "You play very well."

"Thank you. I actually play the piano. The organ has fewer keys, but I manage."

Levi placed his empty plate on the coffee table and then took his coffee mug, "So, what has made you so sad, Abigail?"

Sighing deeply, Abby put her half-eaten piece of pie onto the table also, "You wouldn't believe what I just found out, Levi. It seems my husband was living a double life."

"What? How can that be?" Levi was shocked at the news; what had this man done to his dear Abby.

"My in-laws got a call from a very angry woman claiming that she is the mother of Charlie's fourteen year old daughter, Andrea. She wants money and is planning on giving Andrea up." Abby's eyes teared up again and her shoulders shook.

Levi pulled her against him gently and rubbed her back soothingly, "Ach, what a miserable man you married, Abigail."

"I can't believe he lied to me all those years by keeping such a secret from me. All those business meetings he had said he went to were spent with his daughter." Abby said between racks of sobs.

They sat together holding onto each other for a long time; Levi comforted Abby as she cried. When her cries subsided, she looked up at him, "It seems I've been crying on your shoulder a lot lately. I'm not usually such a cry baby."

"I know," he replied softly, kissing her forehead, just as he had kissed the twins earlier, "What do you plan to do about Andrea?"

"I told the in-laws she could live with me. She was Charlie's child; I owe it to her to take care of her."

Levi brushed her hair with his hand, "Ach, you are such a wonderful gut woman, Abigail. You have captured my heart, just as you will capture hers, I'm sure."

Everyday that week, Levi made sure to call Abby and ask how she was doing. The night of her breakdown, Levi had stayed till she fell asleep in his arms. He had carried her to bed and tucked her in. The next day she asked him why she was in bed in her dress and he just laughed.

Abby relayed to him that Andrea would be coming on the weekend. He grimaced as he thought about what Abby would have to deal with. What kind of mother gave up her daughter? Levi had offered to go with Abby, but she said it would be better if she went alone. Not wanting to upset her, he backed off a little; she had more than enough on her plate as it was.

Chapter Five

Abby meandered around a divider in the airport parking lot, hoping she wasn't too late to pick up Andrea. Chloe and Cole were arguing loudly in the back seat over who would get to help Andrea with her luggage. Frustrated, Abby leaned her arm over the seat and poked them both.

"Okay you two; stop your fighting. I will carry the luggage and you will listen to me." Abby had quite enough of their endless bickering today. It was obvious they were upset with suddenly having a big stepsister sprung on them. She knew how they felt.

A parking spot on the fourth parking lot was just empty and she snuck in it quickly. "Alright kids, you both listen to me. You will stay near me when we go into the busy airport, because it's very easy to get lost in there. Do I make myself clear?"

The twins agreed and followed their mother down the ramp leading to the airport entrance.

"Mommy, is Andrea nice?" Chloe asked, looking up at her mother through squinty eyes, "I sure hope so, cuz she's going to be my step sister."

Abby squeezed her daughter's hand, "I hope so honey. I hope so."

At terminal three, Abby stopped and searched the anxious faces for a lone girl. The only girl who stood out was a brunette dressed in a kilt and pretty blue top; she wore headphones and was flipping through a magazine on a bench. Although she was dressed very prettily, she wore a large scowl on her face.

"Oh, dear." Abby murmured, "It looks like we're in more trouble than I bargained for."

Cole was engrossed in the flight attendants, pilots and the planes he could see through the wall of windows. However, Chloe was looking at the young girl with curiosity.

"Let's see if this girl is Andrea." Abby said, leading the way to the other side of the terminal.

When Cole didn't follow, Abby pulled on his hood, "Come on, Cole. The planes aren't leaving yet, and you can see them just the same over there."

The girl did not look up when they came before her, but merely stared down at an article in the art magazine on her lap.

"Andrea?" Abby inquired bending down to her level.

When she didn't look up, Chloe poked her on her knee, and her head shot up in alarm, "Why did you do that for?" she shouted, not realizing how loud she spoke.

Abby pointed to her earphones and after she pulled them, gingerly off, she spoke up again: "Are you Andrea?"

"That's my name. Are you my Dad's other woman?" she said sharply, fury shooting out of her eyes.

Taking in a deep breath Abby nodded, 'Yes, that's me. How was your trip over?"

"Fine!"

"Listen, I knew as little as you did okay? I didn't know about you or your mother when we married. If I had I would I never had married him. He lied to me too!" Abby said in return, shading the twins behind her.

Andrea bowed her head and than grunted, "Sorry."

"Alright, come on than. Let's get your luggage."

Back at the apartment, Andrea and Abby made a couple of trips back and forth with the luggage and than Abby left her to get settled in her room.

"I know this room isn't very nice right now, it was my office. You can pick out some paint later and we'll make it nice."

Andrea nodded and than shut the door in her face. Abby clenched her fists and made a bear face, "Ugh."

Cole looked up from where he sat coloring at the table, "What's wrong, Mommy?"

"Nothing honey, I'm just a little tired." She yawned enthusiastically and than prepared, a bedtime snack for the twins since it was getting late.

The twins were still getting over the excitement and couldn't stop talking about her at the table. Chloe was jumping up and down in her chair, "Andrea's pretty, hey Mom? Do you think she'll let me borrow her clothes?"

Abby laughed hysterically, "I think you'll have to wait a few years for that, Chloe. You aren't exactly her size."

"Are you going to read to us tonight, Mom?" Cole inquired, taking a slurp from his cocoa, "I want to know what happens next."

Every night during this week, Abby had been reading to the twins from 'The Swiss Family Robinson', since The Charlottes Web was finished." They were right into the story and loved the time spent together in the adventure.

"I'll read the next chapter if you promise to go to sleep right away; no excuses. Deal?"

The twins grinned and shouted happily, "Deal!"

It was over an hour later when Abby was finally able to sit down on the couch with a book. Cole had many questions about the story and Chloe had a tummy ache from all the excitement.

Sighing deeply, Abby settled deeper into the couch and sipped a mug of tea to calm down. She hadn't heard a peep from Andrea's room since they had gotten home and she was worried. Fighting the temptation to inquire after her, she shook her head and started to read.

The grandfather's clock in the hall started to chime at twelve o'clock and Abby jumped up with a start, suddenly awake. She had started getting sleepy after finishing her tea and realized that she had fallen asleep. When she padded into the kitchen, she noticed Andrea's light still on in her room and went to check it out.

"Andrea, are you okay?" she asked at the door. She didn't hear any response so she opened the door quietly and that was when she found her. Andrea sat huddled in a corner of the room crying; her entire body shaking terribly.

Abby sighed, "Oh honey," she said sweetly and than ran over to Andrea's side and sat beside her on the floor, putting an arm around her.

"I have no one to talk to anymore." Andrea cried out, "I am all alone now."

"Don't ever say that, Andrea. I took you in for a reason, okay? You have Chloe, Cole and me now and we're going to take care of you." Abby replied, kissing her on the forehead.

They sat together on the floor for a long time, not saying a word. Inside, Abby's heart felt so sore for the young girl who found herself all alone in the world.

"Would you like some hot cocoa before you go to sleep? It might help you calm down a little after such a busy day!" Abby asked when Andrea's tears had subsided a little.

Andrea nodded and than stood up to follow Abby to the kitchen, "Oh, you just get settled under the covers and I'll bring your drink in here," Abby protested with a wave of her hand.

As she prepared the warm milk, Abby smiled at the progress she had made already. It seemed like everything would be all right after all.

"Get out of my room, you little brat! I don't want you touching my things and I don't want you in here."

Abby, who was just waking up on that Sunday morning groaned at the early banter. She had thought Andrea was getting better on Friday night, but yesterday had been horrible. As usual, the twins got up early and were busy playing in the hallway, when Andrea stormed out of her room and barked at them to keep quiet. Once she slammed the door after retreating to her room, the twins went to Abby scared and sad. When she went to Andrea to tell her to ask politely she just screamed out angrily, "I don't have to listen to you; you're not my Mom."

The entire day had been just as terrible. They went to the park in the afternoon and Andrea sat on a park bench with her nose in a book. While Abby played with Cole and Chloe on the slide, she caught Andrea watching her enviously, and than she scowled and looked back in her book. That night Abby asked Andrea what she felt like having for dinner, and when she got no answer, she opted for pizza. Andrea locked herself in her room, and now was the first time that she had voiced herself again.

Abby crawled out from under the covers and slipped into her pink bunny slippers and robe before walking into the hallway. Chloe sat on the floor outside Andrea's room crying softly, her head on her knees.

"Oh, sweetie, what happened?" Abby asked, bending onto her knees before the upset girl.

Chloe looked up and ran the back of her hand over her eyes, "When I woke up I heard Andrea crying in her room so I knocked on her door and she didn't answer. So I just went in and she was looking at a picture of someone and she was really sad. I went to look at the picture after she put it on her shelf, and she yelled at me."

"Honey, I know you want to be friends with Andrea, but we have to let her have some space. Her Mommy doesn't want to be with her anymore so she's really sad." Abby explained, lightly kissing her daughter on the cheek.

"I would be sad if you left me too, Mommy. Would you ever leave me?"

Abby shook her head, "Never, Chloe. I would never leave you and Cole, and I won't leave Andrea either."

Chloe looked up at her Mother with her big eyes, "Promise?"

"I promise, sweetie."

Just than, Cole came barreling down the hall toward them, "Mommy, Levi's here and he's going to take us to church."

"Oh dear, I'm a mess." Abby scrambled to her feet and touched her hair, which was every which way, "Cole, you keep Mr. Levi company while I get ready okay?"

Before heading back to her room she knocked on Andrea's door, "We're heading to church soon; you better get ready now, alright?"

"Fine," A soft mumble replied from the other side of the door.

Abby smiled to herself as she walked back to her room. Although she tried to be grumpy, Andrea was a softhearted person under it all.

Ten minutes later Abby walked in on a most endearing sight. Levi stood behind Chloe's chair and he was braiding her hair. Chloe was stuffing her face with donuts; clearly, which Levi had brought along.

"Mommy, look. Mr. Levi's braiding my hair."

Abby laughed at the blush on his cheeks, "I see that. He's doing a marvelous job too, maybe you should hire him."

"I wouldn't like anything better, Chloe. You hair is so beautiful." Levi admitted, as he smiled down at her.

After praying, Abby took a homemade donut off the pile on the plate and bit in; they were delicious.

"Did you make these donuts, Levi?"

He nodded, "Yes, I was very excited last night and I couldn't' sleep."

Abby smiled as she licked the icing off her finger, "And you said couldn't bake. They're scrumptious, Levi. I think I could hire you for more than braiding."

Levi laughed as he tied a pink ribbon at the end of Chloe's left braid to match the right and than turned to Abby.

"I'd do it for free, Abby."

"Thank you Levi, you are truly wonderful."

He smiled than and sat down across from her, "So, don't you want to know why I am so excited?"

"Of course, Levi; why are you so excited?"

After taking a sip of the mug of hot coffee before him, he replied earnestly, "I got a job as an assistant to Dr. Larry Fletcher. He's a pediatrician and since I am studying to become one he asked me to join his practice."

Abby jumped up and ran around the table to hug him, not feeling uncomfortable at all, "That's wonderful, Levi. I knew something like this would happen to you. You are such a good man."

Levi laughed and twirled her around, "Jah? You never told me that before."

She swatted him playfully, "Oh you."

Just than, Andrea entered the room with Cole directly behind her. She wore a long flowing skirt and a white blouse, and her hair was pulled back from her face.

"Good morning, Andrea. I'd like for you to meet a good friend of ours, Levi Bontrager." Abby said, as Levi put her back down on her feet. Andrea gave a slight smile and mumbled a greeting as Levi shook her hand.

A half hour later, they were on their way to church and the twins babbled on and on about school and their friends. Andrea was content to just look out of the window at the storefronts and the people milling around.

Levi parked the Bronco nearest to the church and as he hopped out a voice barked from behind him, "Levi, I didn't know you went to this church too."

He turned to be looking directly into the face of his new boss, Dr. Fletcher, "Hello, Larry," Levi said friendlily, "I knew about the job application because I talked to a few of the church members and they pointed you out to me."

Larry Fletcher, a tall and stern looking man, nodded, "Good. I'll see you tomorrow at the office than."

"Jah," Levi said amiably, trying to get a smile from the cold man before he walked away.

"Who was that horrid looking man?" Abby asked as she went to stand beside him.

Levi looked down at her and smiled, "That man is my new boss, Abigail."

Abby blushed prettily, "Oh, I am so sorry…I didn't mean to…"

"No," he interrupted, "You are quite right. He is a rather cold fellow, jah? But, he is supposed to be an amazing physician, and I look forward to working with him."

As they walked up to the church doors Abby noticed Andrea staring at a group of girls her age laughing and talking together as they walked in before them. They stopped talking when they entered the building and snickered. If only she could somehow get Andrea to introduce herself to them.

The service was very interesting; the minister preached whole-heartedly about Ruth and Boaz and Abby knew that the twins would have many questions when they got home. For them to find the hidden meaning in the marriage between Ruth and Boaz was not an easy task to do, they simply took it as a human marriage; not between a regenerated sinner and God.

It was after church when trouble occurred. Levi was talking to

Abby's mother with the twins, when her in-laws noticed Andrea standing beside her.

Gwen Forrester patted on her husbands sleeve and pointed before holding her head high and marching over to them. Andrea paled; obviously, she knew who they were.

"Abby dear," Gwen greeted smoothly, "I see you brought Andrea to church. I hope you will come to your senses and bring her to Social Services so a nice family will take good care of her."

Abby's eyes narrowed in horror and her fists clenched. How dare they speak about their granddaughter in such a rude way; especially straight to her face, "Excuse me? Did I hear you right?"

Roger put an arm around his wife's shoulders, "Abigail, what Gwen is trying to say is that we don't think you'll be about to pay the right amount of attention to Andrea, since you already have the twins to care for."

"You listen to me; Andrea is as much Charlie's child as are Cole and Chloe. She has just as much right to be in our family as we do. You can hardly blame her for her father's indiscretions!"

Gwen paled, "You're blaming our dear Charlie? How could you; he was your husband."

"And he lied to us all. How does that make you feel? He was a drunk throughout our marriage and a liar; and he never loved me the way I loved him."

Roger pulled Gwen away and than said over his shoulder, "I hope you're happy now, Abigail. Gwen is about to swoon from the shock you just gave her."

When they were out of hearing Andrea muttered under her breath, "How rude."

Abby said nothing of the argument after that and went to speak with her mother. Rose knew when her daughter was tense and her eyes held questions, but Abby just shook her head.

Levi dropped them off at home and when Abby asked him in for lunch, he declined saying he had already been invited to his brother's home. Although she was disappointed, Abby gave him a friendly hug goodbye and than watched his truck disappear from view.

Chapter Six

The next days past quickly, with all of the business that Abby had to take care of she had hardly a minute to herself. On Monday, Abby took Andrea over to the Harrisburg High School an hour's drive away. The school headmaster said they took boarders and she was happy to receive her into the school. As they walked back the Bronco, Andrea asked if she had to stay at the school.

"Only if you want to; I'd love to have you stay at home and take the bus. If you make some friends and decide you want to board we can always move you in later." Abby had decided, not wanting Andrea to feel unloved.

Andrea agreed to that immediately, happy to be able to make her own choices. When they got back to Millersburg, Abby took her to a nearby hardware store to pick out paint for her room. She picked out a black and red and also a small can of silver. Abby didn't question the colors, letting her chose her own. While the paint was mixing, Andrea disappeared into a row of art supplies. Abby had noticed her there; and when they were going to pay for the paint, she handed a twenty-dollar bill to Andrea to spend.

She purchased a thick sketchbook, some charcoal, and a pencil kit. Abby smiled and than told her they had to hurry back because Esther was taking over for her in the store.

The following days were better. Andrea started to open up

and she painted modern art on her walls with the colors they had bought. Large swirls swung around the room in artistic delight. Abby complimented Andrea on her talent and the twins pleaded for her to paint their room also. Abby had a few cans of paint in storage left over from the move so she let Andrea use them.

Andrea painted a large butterfly over Chloe's bed and in Cole's a large fire truck with firefighters spraying a burning building. Abby noticed how different she looked when she painted or sketched. Her face glowed with excitement and she was a much happier person.

Abby stirred the pot of spaghetti sauce bubbling in front of her on the gas stove and was broken from her thoughts when the phone rang.

"Andrea, can you get that please?" she called out.

Andrea came around the corner, her hair tied up high on her head with a colorful bandana over it, "Hello," she greeted after picking up the phone.

"Uh huh, she's right here." Andrea handed the receiver to her, not saying who it was.

Abby turned down the element and than held the receiver to her ear, "Hello."

"Abbs?" a deep voice asked.

"Mike?" Abby squealed in delight, jumping up onto her tiptoes with excitement.

He laughed, "How's my favorite sister doing?"

Abby giggled and countered back, "I'm your only sister, silly. How's life in the Navy?"

"I'm home for a month actually; I'm at Mom's right now. I just got in this afternoon; do you think you can come for dinner?"

Again, Abby squealed with delight, "You're here? I'd love to come; oh, but I have dinner on right now. Why don't you come over here instead?"

He sighed, 'Alright, I'll ask Mom."

While he asked their mom, Abby called the twins over and told them their Uncle Mike was home for a while. They jumped up and down shrieking in exuberance.

Mike came back on than and said they would be there in an hour.

Rose was happy to be relieved of making dinner and had immediately agreed to come over.

As soon as she put the phone down Abby asked Andrea to set the table nicely and got the twins to clean up their art supplies and toys. Than, while the noodles and sauce were simmering slowly on the stove she ran to her room to shower. It was almost two and a half years since she had seen Mike and she couldn't wait to see him.

After he had graduated from college, Mike immediately joined the Navy as a Computer Tech. At first, he came home every six months, but when he was offered a promotion, he took it; even though he'd be on the ship longer. He never failed to tell her, however, how much he wanted to be there for her after Charlie's death. Although Mike phoned whenever he could, he was still far away and it was always difficult for Abby to not have him near.

Abby was just combing her hair after a shower when she heard loud excited voices coming from the front entry. As she entered the room a few seconds later she saw her brother swing Chloe up in his arms and give her a giant hug and kiss before putting her down and doing the same to Cole. As he hugged him gently, Mike watched his sister and smiled, than put Cole down.

"You look wonderful, Abbs." Mike announced coming up to engulf her in his big arms. He was a very tall man, over six feet tall with large muscles and a crew cut. Yet his dark hair and blue eyes were just like his sister's.

Abby smiled at Mike and kissed him happily on her cheek, "It's good to see you too, Mike." Than she swatted him playfully across his chest, "How do you keep is such good shape when all you do is sit behind a computer all day."

He laughed, "I work out with a few crew members every day; it makes me feel like I'm actually doing something."

Rose than come up to Abby and hugged her, "How are you doing, Abby dear?"

"I'm feeling better, Mom." Abby exclaimed, before turning to put the dinner on the table. Andrea had set the table with candles and wineglasses for the adults. A beautiful arrangement of flowers in a basket stood magnificently in the center of the table; Andrea had really outdone herself and Abby didn't hesitate to mention it to her.

Mike introduced himself to Andrea and than held her chair out for her. She blushed prettily and thanked him, clearly very smitten with the rough marine.

"Mike, can you ask a blessing for the food?" Abby asked when they were all sitting down around the table.

He obliged and prayed in a calm and reverent voice, so much like his father before him. While they ate, Mike kept them all entertained with stories of his life as a marine.

"We have many serious bits of information on our computers that could cause a huge uproar if someone would be about to hack in to our system," he said, as he reached for the salad bowl, "Once this guy tried to hack into my computer. I was working on government confidential reports and I noticed that someone had snuck in."

Cole, his eyes as round as saucers asked, "Did you catch him Uncle Mike?"

Mike nodded in his direction as he spoke, "Yes, I did. It took a while but we caught him. And do you know how old he was? This guy was only seventeen years old; some men pressured him to work for them and he almost finished doing what they asked. If we wouldn't have noticed the bug, he would probably have been able to do something big with the information. Now he works for us, he's paying off his debts to society this way. Actually, he's down here with me on an assignment."

"Why didn't you bring him along than?" Abby asked as she filled her glass with a vintage red wine.

"He's with a friend tonight, but don't worry you will meet Todd soon enough." He replied, winking at Andrea who again blushed at his teasing manner.

After dinner, they decided to go for a walk and get some ice cream. Mike walked beside Andrea and answered her many questions about the Navy, while Abby walked with her Mother behind the twins.

"Abby dear, what happened at church the other day with Charlie's parents? You looked so upset." Rose inquired, linking her frail arm through her daughters.

Anger flashed through Abby's eyes in remembrance of the horrible fight, "Oh, they were just voicing their opinion on my taking care of

Andrea. And also they claim that their son was not the cause of all the trouble, as usual."

Her mother harrumphed, "Those people wouldn't know the truth if it swung around and nipped them in their rears."

"Mom!" Abby retorted in amazement to her mothers' outburst.

"What? It's true; isn't it? If they think you are the instigator in this madness they have another think coming dear."

Abby shook her head and pulled her Mom closer to her as they walked. It was at times like this that made her thank God for such a wonderful mother. It was no wonder that Charlie turned out the way he was with parents such as his. They spoiled him unconditionally and found no fault in him. So, he grew up knowing he could get away with anything.

By the time, they all returned to the apartment after the ice cream parlor it was long past the twins' bedtime. Andrea took Mike on a tour of the apartment, showing him her newly decorated and furnished room and also the pictures in the twins' rooms. He admired her work and asked if she planned to join any art classes. Andrea told him she hadn't really thought about that but he knew she would consider it now.

Mike and Rose left at ten-thirty and Abby got ready for bed. It was a long time before she fell asleep however, as she thought about the day she had and also about the tall and Amish man that had captured her interest.

On Thursday, Andrea phoned from school to ask if a friend could come over. Abby could tell that she was very excited so she said it was all right. The day had been so crazy in the store with many customers and Abby was still working on the shelves when Andrea got home. The twins were at their grandparents again for the day so it would only be the three of them for dinner.

Andrea walked into the store with a pretty black girl who introduced herself as Kiera Robertson. Her long hair was all braided and her chocolate eyes shone with mischievousness; Abby liked her already.

"There are brownies in the fridge, Andrea. Just make sure your homework is finished before you do anything else, alright?"

"Okay," she responded, before heading up the narrow stairs leading to their apartment.

Abby decided to take a break than and put the bell on the counter for service before heading into the backroom to chat with Esther and Rebecca. The woman had set up the room artistically with quilts draping from the walls and large tables set up for cutting and stitching.

"How is business going ladies?" Abby asked as she strolled around the room, gazing at the different patterns on each design.

Rebecca, the blond woman with large green eyes, did not look up from her work as she responded, "As well as can be imagined, ain't so Esther?"

"Jah; we are doing alright. But I think we should mayhap put a sign up front as well to attract more customers. Is that alright, Abigail?"

Abby walked over to Esther's table and observed as she arranged the quilt pieces in the correct order, "Sure, that's a great idea. Do you have any name picked out for your business?"

"Jah," Rebecca announced with a bright smile, "The Quilting Bee."

"That's a very interesting name; I'm sure you will do well with it."

Esther sight, "I'm just afraid of what Thomas will say about it all. He didn't mind much when we just started, but now he's been very hesitant."

"It is the same with Seth; he doesn't want me to spend so much time here. He says a woman's place is in the home." Rebecca murmured, standing up to eye her work from afar.

"Do you think it is a good idea to put the sign up out front than? I wouldn't want tension to come in between your relationships." Abby prepared a mug of coffee for herself from the pot in a corner as she spoke, "Maybe you should just make your quilts here and than sell them at the Farmers Market."

"Jah that is a very good idea." Esther agreed, "We can get other wives to come and help also."

As the two women started planning for a quilting bee, Abby

retreated to the store just as she heard the service bell ring three times.

"Levi," she called out in excitement as she found her new friend at the counter with his coat over an arm.

He smiled, his brown eyes twinkling down at her, "Gut daag, Abigail."

Abby went up and gave him a hug, "It's so good to see you again. How is everything going with school and your new job?"

"It is going really well actually. I have an hour off so I though I'd come and see you." He seemed edgy even though he smiled, and he fidgeted with his hands as he spoke.

Pulling him along behind her, Abby pushed him onto a chair at the coffee table, "You look beat, mister. Have a seat while I get some tea and cookies; just rest here awhile."

When she came back a few minutes later holding a tray laden with mugs of tea and a plate of sugar cookies, he sat with his head on his arms at the table. Levi looked up when she set the tea before him; his eyes were weary and his face pale.

"Are you going to tell me what's bothering you? Or do I have to guess?" Abby asked as she sat across from him, folding her legs before her.

He closed his eyes as he sipped the tea and sighed, "I guess I'm just very tired, I went to bed early last night but I got called to assist at an emergency a little after midnight. Dr. Fletcher is no pushover for latecomers and he showed his displeasure by making me do mundane tasks the entire night."

Abby could tell he spoke the truth, yet she knew he wasn't telling the entire truth. However, she did not question him, for she knew he'd tell her when he was ready.

"My brother Mike came home on Tuesday from the Navy. He's staying at Mom's right now."

Levi nodded, "Jah, I know. I was at your mother's home yesterday."

"Really; why?" Abby asked, her eyes showing puzzlement.

He grinned, "Her sink got backed up, and Mike couldn't unclog it; so she called me. She said she'd pay me with cinnamon buns and I just couldn't pass that up."

Abby laughed than, happy to see he was loosening up a little, "Of course you couldn't; Mom makes the best cinnamon buns in the world."

"Your brother is an amazing man, Abby. He's been all over the world and the pictures he takes are magnificent. I always wanted a digital camera, but I never know which to buy."

She nodded at that remark, "Yes, he is a very accomplished photographer. When we went on vacation as kids he'd be out for hours taking nature pictures while the rest of us swam and hiked."

Levi took a cookie off the plate and popped it into his mouth. After he finished it he grinned, "These are great. Hey, where are the twins and Andrea?"

"Andrea is upstairs with a friend and the twins are with their grandparents."

He looked at his watch and grimaced, "I have to be in class in fifteen minutes so I'd better get going. Thanks for the tea."

"It was my pleasure; you better have some rest after your class." She said smartly as he walked towards the door.

"Okay, mother hen," he said with a wink.

Abby swatted him playfully, "Hey, I am not a mother hen, I just worry about you."

"I know. It is nice that you care, Abigail." He touched her cheek softly and than said goodbye.

It was an hour before closing and Abby had nothing left to do. So she swept the floor for a second time, rechecked her inventory and than went to her computer to work on her bookkeeping. When it was near closing time, she called up Pablo's Pizzeria and ordered two large pies; knowing it would be too much to eat.

Chapter Seven

The October night was crisp as Levi headed into the private hospital, hosted by Doctors Larry Fletcher and Mort Welling. He tucked his hands into his long winter coat to keep warm as he ducked his head to ward off the slight wind. Larry had called him in a state of frantic, saying he needed someone to cover for him while he attended to some urgent business. This was not the first time this had occurred and Levi was putting more hours in than any assistant would normally have to.

As he walked through the swinging doors, a bubbly nurse greeted him from behind the reception desk and whisked him through. Dr. Fletcher sat on the edge of a small frail girl's bed as he checked her vitals. Levi stood by as he examined her.

"Alright Jodie; it looks like you'll be staying a few days longer. Your heart isn't as strong as we want it to be yet. If you stay here we can monitor your heart rate and keep a close watch." He announced in a brisk manner, clearly in a hurry.

He looked up at Levi and than stood up, "This is my assistant, Resident Dr. Bontrager and he'll be here if you have any questions or if you want company."

The little girl smiled up at him through thick eyelids, "Hello," she croaked hoarsely.

"Hello Jodie. If you need me you just push the button beside you okay?" Levi said sweetly, drawing her blanket up to her chin. She nodded gingerly and settled down to go to sleep.

Levi walked with Larry to the front entrance where the room was filled with patients waiting eagerly, "Listen," he explained, "I know that you probably think it's strange that I am leaving all the time, but I'll make it up to you. The clinic may need some help tonight, so be on alert if they call, all right? I don't think Dr. Welling is going to be able to handle things on his own."

After his supervisor left, Levi went to the receptionist's desk and looked over the patient blog up on the north wall. For the past three days, he had doctored the same patients. Patients that should have been gone long ago, according to the medical notes. He sighed and thought better than to be caught up in the reasons for his supervisor's medical standards and took the first chart off the counter.

It was over two hours later before he finished the rounds and was called to the clinic. He was surprised at the amount of patients still waiting to be addressed; so he told the receptionist to speed things along and help the patients as efficiently as possible.

After his third clinical patient for the evening, a young man about the age of seventeen waited for him in one of the observation rooms. His face was very pale and his eyes watery from the pain.

"Hey, where is the doc at?" he asked with a snarl in his voice.

"I'm the Resident, Doctor Bontrager. What can I do to help?" Levi sat down across from the patient, putting the patients file down on the small table. The name of the young man was Neil Thompson, and he had come in a few days back with stomach pain. Dr. Fletcher had given him pain medication and a prescription for anti-acids and told him to come back if it got worse.

Neil groaned and thrust a hand through his curly hair, "I've been having really bad pain, ya know? And the other Doc said that he had some good pills to help with it. He said that they were just new and that he couldn't prescribe them; he gave me some samples from the office."

Levi frowned and swiveled his chair towards Neil, "That's strange; there are no samples here that are a new product. Why don't you lay back and I'll take a look at your stomach, okay?"

As his patient lay down on the doctors table, Levi inwardly

contemplated the strange actions of his supervisor. But, seeing as Neil was his first priority, he shook the thoughts from his mind and set to examining him.

"Alright," he exclaimed after a few seconds of probing and Neil's screams in pain, "It looks like it isn't your stomach at all Neil; it seems to be appendicitis. We're going to have to run a few tests to find out for sure, but all the signs point to it."

A beautiful Asian nurse came in than and Neil was happy to go along for the tests as he left the room smiling. Levi however, took the packet of samples Neil had handed over and went to the lab.

"Are you absolutely sure about this Elizabeth? This is no time for mistakes you know."

Levi sat across from the lab nurse who had just handed him the result from the content of the pills. The screen they had run on them claimed to be a few vitamins, such as vitamin A, B, and a few endorphins; nothing that could heal a patient with a supposed stomach ulcer.

Elizabeth glared down at Levi with her hands on her broad hips, "Doctor Bontrager, never underestimate the power of science. Of course that diagnosis is correct; I studied for three years for a reason you know."

"Alright," he stood up and put the sheets in his file, "well, thanks for the help. I'll just have to have a talk with Doctor Fletcher about this I guess."

Levi went to the receptionist's desk and handed the nurse at the station the file, "Could you put this somewhere safe, Arlene? This is valuable information and I'll need it when the shifts done; I just don't want to lose it."

Arlene nodded and ran a hand through her bright orange hair, "That's not a problem Doctor B. You know, you're getting quite the reputation around here."

Smiling, he leaned over the counter down at her, "Really; and what is the word around here?"

"Word is that you are the kindest, most sincere doctor to grace these halls since its opening," she said with a slight whisper, "Isn't that something?"

"Jah, that sure is." Levi smiled again and than stood up straight, "Well, I better continue on than; I wouldn't want to disgrace the patients."

The next few patients needed treatment for minor issues; like a cough, a terrible stomach ache, and a cut on a child's finger. Although they were just negligible things, they were the ones that gave Levi the most headaches. When his break finally came at three o'clock; Levi went into the lunchroom and ate his snack in complete silence. But, as he was just finishing his apple, the door burst open and the Asian nurse from before called out to him frantically.

"You've got to come, Doctor B. That young boy with the stomach pain; he's throwing up everywhere and we can't get a decent picture."

Throwing the apple core in the garbage and picking up his file, Levi followed her down the hall to the x-ray rooms. It was not a pretty sight to see Neil bending over and convulsing terribly. Levi went to his side and put in an IV, "Get me some Gravel and Morphine STAT," he ordered to the nurse, "Let's get Mr. Thompson a little more comfortable. And get some one to call his parents."

Levi stayed by Neil's side until he fell asleep and than went out while a nurse cleaned up all the mess. *What a night*, he thought to himself, running a hand through his hair, *I can't believe I am doing all this without Dr. Fletcher; this doesn't seem right. He should be here for this, directing me on what to do. And what's this about a new medication that cures stomach pain with vitamins?* Shaking his head in wonder, Levi went to the phone and decided to give Dr. Larry Fletcher a call.

The phone rang four times before it was answered by a chirpy female, "Fletcher residence," she said with a giggle. Levi heard Larry's voice in the background telling her to hand him the cell phone.

"Who is this?" he asked with a snarl.

"Levi Bontrager, we're having a problem down here at the clinic and I really think you should be down here."

"Tell me what's going on!" Larry ordered.

Levi ran a hand down his face and sighed, "A patient came in by the name of Neil Thompson, claiming to have been here three days ago with stomach pain. His file states that you gave him anti acids and pain meds, but he tells me that you gave him some samples that are being promoted right now."

"Yes, the Miracure. It's my new medication to help fight infections." Larry explained dryly, "Why did the patient return?"

"He has appendicitis sir, and we need to operate right away. But, with you gone and the other doctor busy with other patients I need you here."

Larry groaned loudly, "Listen Bontrager, I am a bit tied up right now so I'm going to need you to take care of it. Don't worry you'll be marked high for cooperation."

Levi was just about to tell him what he had found out about Miracure but Larry had hung up on him already. Sighing, he lay the receiver down and turned to Trichelle, the name of Neil's nurse, "I guess we prep him for surgery, jah?"

The sound of an alarm clock ringing near his head woke Levi up from his deep sleep. The flashing numbers read 6:30, and Levi had to be at work at twelve tonight. First, he wanted to do some research on the Miracure promotion and eat a good supper. He stretched and yawned at the same time, and than padded his way to the washroom. As he brushed his teeth the sound of the phone ringing in the kitchen made him jump, and he ran towards it reluctantly.

"Hello there, Levi. How are things going for your residency?" It was his old boss Todd.

Smiling, Levi cradled the phone by his ear and opened the fridge to see what he could possibly make for dinner, "Hello Todd. Checking up on me, are you? I'm doing gut; how's the family?"

"Things have been great with the family, but I really miss you at work. The guys are not very dependable with you gone; I wish you could have stayed, Levi." Todd sounded about down to his last thread.

Levi took out some veggies for a salad and started cutting them on a board, "Jah, I wish I could split myself in two, Todd. Things have been really crazy for me too."

"Well, why don't you come down for dinner? Beth's made a huge meal and my brother Sean is over too."

Since Todd sounded like he really needed someone to talk to,

Levi asked if he could bring a salad and than hung up the phone to get ready. After taking a quick shower and dressing up in his new grey wool slacks and a dusty blue pull-over, Levi headed out to the Landers country home on the east side of town.

He always enjoyed the drive there because the feeling of home always surrounded him. In order to get to Todd's home, he had to pass through the main Amish community; the school, the meeting hall for special occasions and many of the farms. During this trip he often stopped to talk to friends as they walked by, it was his only chance of talking to them.

Finally, after virtually a half hours drive, he pulled into the Landers laneway and parked behind Sean's Subaru. Todd and Beth's two daughters, Meg and Tania ran from the house and grabbed him around the knees.

"Gut daag, girls! You better watch, or you'll be tossed in with the salad." He winked down at them and carefully walked up the steps behind them.

The two girls giggled and opened the door happily. Beth and Sean's wife Susan were setting the table in the dining room and they gestured for him to put the salad in the center.

"Hey, there he is!" a deep familiar voice exclaimed from the kitchen doorway. Todd Landers walked across the room and gave him a big manly hug, "It's good to see you, Levi."

Levi laughed and slapped him playfully on the back, "It's nice to see you to, Todd."

"Before you guys head off to play pool in the rec room, you better sit down and eat." Beth advised, leading them to the table.

Todd rolled his eyes and looked over his shoulder at Levi, "She isn't usually this bossy, you know. Sometimes I actually get a word in edgewise."

After prayer, everyone dug into the meal and chatted about their day. Beth had turned some of Todd's laundry pink when she accidentally threw in one of Tania's shirts with his. Todd had taken out his crew for breakfast and Levi joked that he wished he were still working for him. Than, Sean talked about a case at work and how he was up for promotion to chief of police. Everyone congratulated him on his achievement and than they were interrupted by the doorbell ringing.

"That must be Lori. She said she'd be over to show me the new designs for the Rec Center." Todd exclaimed, jumping from his seat to greet her at the door. Levi knew Lori Schelling from when his wife was still alive. She had been her best friend so Levi saw a lot of her during the week. While his wife had been alive, she had confided in him about Lori's issues with men, so Levi ended up knowing her as good as his wife.

"Levi?" A loud shriek came from the doorway, taking him back to the present. Lori stood beside Todd, looking just the same as the last time he had spoken to her. Her red hair was pulled back from her face slightly and the rest framed her face in layers. She wore the same dark glasses and smile that he remembered.

Levi stood up and walked around the table until he stood before her, "It's good to see you too, Lori." He gave her a friendly hug and than was surprised when she clung onto him a little longer than necessary.

"I can't believe it's you? You're accent is almost gone now, and you look so happy," Lori took a seat at the table beside him as she spoke.

"Well, it has been two years since we last saw each other, jah? What have you been up to lately? Is there a man in your life?"

Lori blushed and looked away for a moment; Levi grew uncomfortable with this new Lori, "No, there are no men in my life. I have just been working steady and aiming for a promotion."

"Well, it's good to see you're doing well. However, I really need to speak to Todd before you take over and we need to pray yet."

Levi didn't mean to be so abrupt, but he knew that once Todd and she got started on the plans he would never get a chance to speak to him about Miracure. After prayer, Todd took Levi to his office where they stretched out with their legs on the desk, both on opposite sides.

"It feels so good to get away from the crowd; I have too much on my mind right now." Todd exclaimed, putting his hands behind his head, "Lori is here with new plans for the Rec center on the other side of Churchville. A few months ago, I signed on with this architect, Andre Puter, and he said that I could start working for him next year.

Now, all of a sudden he tells me that if I want to work for him still I have to start for him now. But, I am completely booked full until next year." He groaned, "Levi, I just don't know what to do. By working for Andre, I could make more on this one project than what I will in the entire year otherwise. Yet, if I cancel all the other jobs, I'll just lose my reputation and the valued customers."

Levi sat up and clasped his hands together, "Why don't you hire a few more men and split them up? Michael is a great supervisor; you could train him to work on his own with some of the men. That way, you could do both jobs, get double the money, and still keep your reputation in tact. Gut idea, jah?"

"Okay, that makes sense. But, Michael has been saying that he doesn't really want to have the responsibility anymore because the other men are not listening to him." Todd opened a file folder and pulled out a few sheets of paper, "Just last week, two of the men took off at lunch to eat out without telling him, and they were supposed to meet me at a new job site."

"Why don't you offer him a raise? I know that for a while you will have a hard time financially, but after the first check you will have made it all back."

He nodded, "That's true. Levi, you should be the boss of this company, not me. It seems that you have all the ideas tonight."

Levi chuckled and shrugged sheepishly, "I guess I'm just glad to be helping out a friend. I could never live my life being a construction worker, Todd. My life is all about people and helping them; without that I am nothing."

"I know; I just wish you really like construction as much as being a doctor."

"Well, I'm afraid that sometimes I wish just the same." Levi admitted, leaning back in his chair, "I just found out that my supervisor, Dr. Larry Fletcher, has made a new medicine called Miracure. This medication, however, is a total sham; when I got the lab to check it out we found vitamins and some other minor ingredients. There was nothing even substantial to a miracle."

Todd raised his eyebrows in surprise, "Wow; did you confront him about it?"

Grimacing, Levi shook his head, "He hung up the phone before

I could. I had called him because the patient I was seeing needed an emergency appendectomy; and he told me to do it myself. Strange, huh?"

"You should talk to Sean about this, maybe he can help investigate." Todd stood up and went out to call his brother, who was washing dishes in the kitchen with his wife.

Sean came into the office and sat beside Levi, asking questions about what he had discovered and if he had any evidence pertaining to the crime.

"I have the results from the lab at the hospital; I can call the receptionist and ask her to bring it over right away."

However, when he called Arlene and asked for the file she claimed she couldn't find it. She had put it in a safe drawer, went for coffee and now it was gone. Groaning, Levi thanked her anyway and hung up. The three men talked for a while longer about the options that he had and than Levi realized it was time to head on home. He had to work the night shift again, and he needed to pack a lunch and change.

Chapter Eight

Later that night, as Levi was hanging up his coat in his locker and putting his lunch in the staff refrigerator, he heard raised voices coming from the conference room in the back. Feeling a little ashamed to be listening in, he strode to the back of the room and hid behind a row of lockers.

Levi recognized the strained voice of his supervisor speaking, "I don't care if you have to get them to sign the papers at gunpoint, Alan, just get it done. We don't have much time left before the promotion of Miracure. Investors will be there handing out money, company's will sign up with us and we will be millionaires within a few days. So, just do what you have to."

Alan, the target of the conversation blubbered impatiently, "I don't have the authority to get the health officials to sign, Larry, and you know it. If I do anything rash, they are likely to arrest us."

"Listen to me, Alan. I have helped you get to the height of your career; so it is now your turn to help me get to mine. If you do not help me with this, I will personally ruin your career with my bare hands. Do you understand?"

From his spot behind the lockers, Levi gasped in horror at the evilness coming out of Larry. He had always known that he was a scary man, but he had never imagined this. Levi prayed silently to God, asking Him to change Larry's heart to the better. Than he asked for strength, courage and safety while he tried to gain evidence. It was too bad to that he did not have a tape recorder with him; but life was not that easy.

Alan than exclaimed that he would do everything in his power to make the men sign the papers, even though Levi could tell that he was hesitant. He than exclaimed to Larry something that made Levi's heart stop.

"I heard from a friend in the lab that your little friend has been poking his nose in our business. He supposedly took some of the Miracure pills to the lab to be analyzed."

"He what?" Larry screamed, pounding his fist against something hard, "How did this happen?"

His companion snorted, "Obviously he isn't as dumb as you think. He had the results hidden in the receptionist's desk. I made sure to get rid of it and any other samples of the medication."

"Good. I don't want to hear any more of this guy ruining our plans."

Levi quickly shrugged into his lab coat and walked down the long hallway to the children's ward. He wanted to be as far away from the men as possible; this was getting too close for comfort.

When he got to the front desk to get the patient files for his rounds, he spotted the familiar backside of a woman chatting to the receptionist. His stomach churned when she turned around and Lori Schelling looked back at him with a bright smile on her face.

"Hello Levi, I realize we didn't have time to talk at Todd's place, so I came over to see you."

Levi groaned inwardly, "You want to talk with me *now*? I'm just starting my shift and I'm late as it is. Plus, you must know that I'm seeing someone who is pretty special to me."

Lori waved a hand as if sweeping his comment away, "Oh please Levi, I just want to talk. I never said anything about getting together; you were my best friends' husband."

"Okay, I'm sorry. Why don't you meet me at the cafeteria tomorrow morning when I get off work? That is, if you really want to talk." He secretly hoped she would get the point and leave it at that.

However, that was not what she had in mind, "Alright, that sounds good," she exclaimed brightly, "I'll see you in the morning. Don't work to hard, okay?"

She left him leaning on the counter as she waltzed away, waving over her shoulder dramatically. Somehow, Levi did not think that she meant what she said about her not wanting to date him. It was obvious that the woman had been flirting with him.

Back in the locker room ten hours later, Levi shrugged out of his lab coat and grabbed his wallet before heading to the crowded cafeteria. He spotted Lori right away sitting in the corner reading. Levi waved in her direction when she looked up and pointed to the buffet. He piled his plate full of sausages, eggs, and pancakes and than made his way towards her. At least he would be able to eat; it would limit the talking.

"You look hungry." She exclaimed, "You must not have listened to my advice."

Levi frowned, uncertain of what she meant, "Huh?"

She rolled her eyes, "Come on Levi, you aren't that dense are you? I told you not to work too hard."

"Oh, that. Jah, well, its difficult not to work hard in a place like this." He went on to talk about some of the patients he had that night and she nodded along patiently. After a while, he asked if he could pray for his food and she obliged.

"So," she asked after he finished, "How have things been going with that Miracure episode? I heard about it from Todd; he was really worried."

Levi shifted uncomfortably, "He told you about that?"

Smiling, Lori leaned over, picked up a piece of sausage with a fork, and popped it into her mouth, nodding as she chewed.

Anger burst within him, and Levi tried to calm himself down. He didn't like people eating off his plate, especially someone who he hardly knew. Now, Abby…well she could eat off his plate anytime. Shaking the thoughts from his mind, Levi than explained to her that nothing substantial had happened since than. It wasn't any of her business to know what he had witnessed that morning. Especially since he hadn't told Sean yet.

Lori was just leaning over to take another piece of sausage when a voice behind him spoke up quietly, "Hello Levi."

He turned to see Abby standing there holding her jacket in her arms and his heart leapt. She looked so beautiful; radiant actually, except for the puzzlement shown on her face, "Hi Abby, what are you doing here?"

She blushed prettily, "I just wanted to stop in and see if you wanted breakfast. But it looks like you're already eating so I'll just leave."

"Leave? Don't do that Abby; I would love to spend time with you. Why don't I finish up here and than we can talk?"

Her gaze went from him to Lori who was chewing on the sausage and looking back and forth between them, "No, that's okay. I'll leave you two alone; I have things to do anyway." In addition, before he could change her mind, she was gone.

"I'm sorry Lori, but I have to catch up with Abby. Thanks for the talk." He stood up and ran down the hallway after her. It wasn't long before he saw the edge of her skirt disappearing around a corner.

"Abby, wait up; I need to talk to you." He called out loudly, hoping she would stop just so he'd quiet down. When he came around the next corner, he nearly ran directly into her.

Her eyes were brimming unshed tears and her face looked pained and pale, "What do you want, Levi. I have things that need doing."

Sighing, Levi took her gently by the arms, "I know that looked bad back there, but Lori was the best friend of my wife and I met her at Todd's last night. She just wanted to talk, and if she wanted more… well, she couldn't have me. It happens that I really like this gorgeous woman, a single mother and friend who I would like to officially date."

"That's okay, Levi. It's not as if we're dating right now anyways. You can talk to whomever you want; I don't have a say." She started to walk away from him than, but he ran and stood before her.

"I want you to listen to me, really listen; okay?" he looked deep into her dark eyes, "Ever since I first saw you in the bookstore on that day, I have felt that you have changed my life so significantly. I was barely living before you came into my life. Abby, I really need you to be in my life; and it's not just about me. It seems that you really want to be with me too. Jah?"

Abby nodded cautiously, "Yes, but when I saw you with that woman back there I got scared. Did you know she was eating off your plate?"

Levi allowed himself to laugh, "Uh huh, although it really made me mad. I don't like sharing food off my plate to strangers." He scrunched his face up, "Does that make me selfish?"

"No, you just know what you want. I know that if you were in a room full of starving people, you would feed them every crumb off your plate. It is just annoying, when people who have a full plate in front of them eat off others plates as well. It's called gluttony." She weaved her arm through his and they walked to the front entrance where Levi kissed her lightly on the forehead and than helped her into her Bronco.

Chapter Nine

Two days later, Abby stared out from her kitchen window at the bright sunlight illuminating in the sky. Ever since her talk with Levi that day, she had felt horrible about her suspicions of him and Lori. Once they had talked it over, they decided to let things rest and continue with their relationship. Nevertheless, it was hard for Abby to think about Levi with other woman. She never really thought about him having girls who liked him; to her he was just an average looking man. However, when she saw him with that woman, she saw him in a completely new light. He was no longer average looking; now he was looking great and happy. No longer did she think of him as a lonely man, but a man that is trapped by those women who run hesitantly around him trying to get his attention.

The phone rang from its holder on the wall beside her, and Abby picked it up as she watched a man across the street watering his petunias on the patio.

"Hello, Abby speaking," she said with a soft voice.

"Abby, it's Levi. I just wanted to see what you all are doing today. I have something planned as an apology. That is, if you will accept it."

Abby was happy to hear his voice, "Well, the kids really want to get out, so that would be great. What do you have planned?"

He chuckled huskily, "You'll just have to wait; it's a surprise."

"Oh," she smiled than, "What time will you be here?"

"Be ready in an hour, okay?"

She agreed and than as she said goodbye, Andrea walked sleepily into the room rubbing her eyes. "Who was that?" she inquired.

"Levi, he's taking us all out for the day and he'll be here in an hour so you better wake up the twins and get ready," she advised, rushing past her to her room to change.

An hour later, Abby was drinking her coffee at the kitchen table dressed in a long jean skirt and a burgundy frilly top with a matching necklace. Andrea had helped her chose the outfit because she thought that the outfit she picked out was 'lame'. Abby was finding out that Andrea was a major drama queen. She was funny, artistic, and very stylish. She helped the twins with their homework whenever she could, and made her own jewelry for them too. They just loved her as Abby was starting too.

"Levi's here!" Cole called from the front window, "I can't wait to see where he's taking us."

Levi came in a few seconds later with a big grin on his face, "Gut daag everyone. Are we all ready to go now?"

From where she sat at the table, Abby smiled his way and nodded, "Yes, we are. Andrea is just finishing Chloe's hair and we will be ready to take off."

"Gut; this is really going to be a wonderful-gut day. Wait until you see where we will be going."

They all packed up into the Bronco and Levi transferred some paper bags from his truck. Than they were off down the I-90, kid's music was blaring from the stereo system and the twins bobbing their heads to the music. Even Levi sang along with some of the songs, and Cole and Chloe would giggle and sing loud too. Abby just liked to watch him with her children and listen to his low voice singing the children songs.

Suddenly, Abby realized that they were turning off by the road leading to Abe and Libby's home. She tried to brainstorm ideas as to what the surprise might be, but it was hard to think when the children were laughing and singing so loudly. Levi turned to her as he sang and winked brightly her way. Immediately she could feel her face turn hot and she placed her hands on her cheeks. He started to laugh than, and took one of her hands in his own, squeezing it gently.

"When are we going to stop Levi? I have to go to the bathroom real bad." Cole exclaimed, jumping up and down on his seat.

Levi grinned into the rear view mirror, "We'll be stopping soon Cole, but you better keep your bottom on the seat or you might not make it."

Abby liked the way he disciplined; it was firm yet open. Moreover, she could tell that the children respected him more for it, especially the twins. Charles had been a very loud and harsh disciplinarian, and the children had crawled deep into their shells when he was around. It took a long time before they came out of them after his death.

When the Bontrager Farm came into view, Cole and Chloe bounced up and down in excitement, "Do I get to play with Olivia?" Chloe asked.

"No, we are only stopping for a little bit." Levi announced, turning the Bronco into the long laneway, "I have to run across the street to Marta Zook's place first. While I do that, you can all use the outhouse and than go in to Libby."

Once the vehicle came to a full stop, Cole and Chloe jumped out and ran for the outhouse. Andrea, however, stood back with Abby and turned her head in embarrassment when Levi softly kissed Abby on the cheek. Abby blushed again and watched as he ran down the laneway to the road.

"Do you love Levi?" Andrea asked, walking a little closer to where Abby stood near the Bronco.

Abby laughed nervously, "I don't think I know him well enough to answer that, sweetheart."

Andrea frowned and twirled a strand of hair around her finger, "Oh, I was just wondering because one of my friends from school is dating an older guy. They've only been dating a few weeks but she says she loves him. I told her she's crazy, but she said that when you find that right person than it all just works."

"How old is her boyfriend, Andrea?" Abby asked inquisitively. A girl of fourteen talking about relationships in that manner did not sound right.

After pausing a minute to think, she responded carefully, "I think he's twenty-one or something. He goes to the college nearby and she met him at the diner where she works."

"Twenty-one years old? Do her parents know about this?"

"That's the problem; she's in foster care and they don't care what she does, as long as she gives part of her check to them every month."

Abby could tell that Andrea was very worried about her friend, and that meant that they were close. She put her arm around Andrea and they walked toward the backdoor, where Libby was letting the twins in, "Listen, why don't you invite her over for dinner some night this week and I'll talk to her? Would that be okay? I won't pry; I'll just ask questions that are normal."

"Okay, but let her do the talking."

"Alright," Abby replied as they walked up the steps.

Libby held the door open for them and led them into the warm kitchen where young Abe and Olivia sat making cookies. The twins instantly went to their aid and Andrea hesitantly went over to join them, leaving the adults to talk in the living room.

"So, how are you doing, Abigail?" Libby asked, settling down in a rocker, "I haven't spoken to you in a while and I thought their must be something wrong."

Abby smiled and shook her head, "Oh no, everything has been great. The Bookworm has been getting new customers every week, and the twins are doing very well in school. Andrea has joined an art class at the college, I'm a little scared about that but she seems to be responsible."

"I hear tell that our Levi is giving you a surprise today," her friend announced, than smiling as she looked out the window she said, "And it looks like your first one is on its way down the lane."

Giggling, Abby ran to the window to see what was coming. She sighed when she saw Levi coming down the lane in a black buggy, dressed in the clothes of his former community. He looked wonderful.

"You better come and see what Levi has done everyone, it sure is a surprise."

Soon everyone ran out the back door and Levi held up two bags as he jumped down from the buggy, "So, what do you think about it?"

The twins cheered and jumped up and down, and Andrea went

over to inspect the inside. However, he was much more interested in Abby's reaction. Abby realized that he was only looking at her and not the children, she smiled and whispered, "thank you," over their heads.

"I've got some bags here with clothes for each of you to wear. Today we are having a typical Amish day, without all the work of course." Levi handed out the clothes, and Libby showed the twins how to dress in them. Abby went up to the spare room and put on the plain long navy skirt, white blouse and bonnet. Than she tied a pale blue apron around her waist and went down to see the rest of the clan.

"Mommy, I look just like Olivia!" Chloe exclaimed, running towards her with open arms.

"Yes, you certainly do, my dear," Abby retorted, hugging her daughter close. Her dark curly hair was now hidden behind a blue bonnet and her matching dress held a small apron on the front. Cole, who was still getting help from Levi with the buttons on his shirt, looked equally adorable. He even had the black hat and suspenders on.

Levi stood up than and looked at each of them with a wide smile, "Jah, you all look like Amish to me." He than turned to his sister who was looking at them all with shining eyes, "What do you think, Elizabeth?"

She smiled and straightened Cole's hat, "Jah, they'll do just fine, brother."

Andrea, who was standing off to the corner trying to get her bonnet to work, suddenly spoke up, "Why are we all dressing up? What's so interesting about this?"

"Andrea," Abby said curtly, "don't talk like that. Levi has out done himself to share with us a little about the life of the Amish. Very few people like us actually get to be inside their homes, so this is very special."

"I wasn't being rude, Mom, I just wanted to know the reason for dressing up?" Andrea said flippantly, turning to Libby for help.

Abby's breath caught in her throat, it was the first time Andrea had called her Mom. "Do you really think of me as your mother?"

Tears came to Andrea's eyes, but she looked down ashamed, "Well, my real mother doesn't want me and you took me in. I just thought that since I don't have a real mother any more maybe you could be mine."

"I would love to be your mother Andrea!" Abby met her 'daughter' in stride and hugged her tight, sobbing joyously as she did so, "Oh, I am so happy honey."

All the adults looked at each other with tears in their eyes, and than Levi led them all out to the buggy. He had put blankets, hot chocolate, and a camera to take pictures, and some books for the children. Than, to Abby's surprise, Libby came outside with a basket full of Amish food. After thanking her for everything, the children climbed into the buggy and Abby hopped up beside Levi on the front.

"It might get a little cold out here, but I put some blankets up front here so we can cuddle up. There's also hot chocolate in the box beside you, so we can have some after," he exclaimed as they rode down the drive.

Abby leaned against his broad shoulder, "Levi, I thank God everyday for letting you come into my life. You have given me another reason to get up every morning. Before you come into my life, I was very miserable. After my husband's death, I became very drawn and unhappy. The only happiness I had was with the twins, but now I am happy about so much more."

Levi put an arm around her shoulders and squeezed her gently toward him, "Aah Abigail, I was just the same before I met you. Now, my whole life has changed."

They rode along in silence for a while and than Abby asked him about how he left the community and he politely told her the details of what had happened.

"I had first met Sarah when I was working at the lumber mill in town over the summer. Her father was a frequent buyer and I had to help him often with loading up his truck. Sometimes, Sarah would come along with him and we would talk. At first I was hesitant, but than I just thought that she was also a customer so it would be alright." Levi cracked the reins and the horses sped up a little.

"Over time, we started to talk longer and I would take her for rides in my buggy. I knew it was wrong but it felt so right. During these rides, Sarah would talk about the God she knew and the life she lived. And I grew curious, of course, and one Sunday I told my father that I was going to church with Sarah and her family. He was mad, but since it was Rumspringe, he had little to say about my decision. That first Sunday in church, I felt closer to God than I had ever felt in my entire life as an Amish boy. When we sang together I realized that there was much more to life than the little community I was so used to."

Abby looked up at him and watched as he concentrated on the road ahead and the story he was telling. His face gave away the emotions he felt as he spoke, and right now, she could tell that it had been a life-changing event.

"Sarah and I announced our engagement two months later, and my parents were outraged. They had not thought that our relationship would get so deep, but we loved each other and I wanted to leave the community with her. After a few months, we got married in Sarah's church with her family as witnesses," he looked down at her than and said, "But what really surprised me, was when Abe came into the church to see the ceremony. He got in real trouble from my father but he has always told me that he never regretted coming to see me get married."

Abby snuggled close to his side and sighed deeply, "That must have taken a lot of strength to come. Did you ever see your father after that?"

"I have seen him, yes. But we have not talked since the day I left the community."

For a while, they rode in silence and just enjoyed the slow moving scenery around them. From inside the buggy, Abby could here Andrea reading to the twins in an exaggerated voice. It felt nice to sit quietly and yet enjoy Levi's company; they never really got the chance to do that and she now she seemed more drawn to him than ever before.

It wasn't much longer when they came to a fork in the road and Levi turned off on the narrower of the two. Abby couldn't hide her inquisitiveness and kept asking him questions about where they were going. He only told her that she was not very good with surprises and she admitted that she wasn't. When they came up to a wooden gate that crossed the road, Levi hopped down from the buggy and opened it before leading the horses and the buggy through to the other side. After he had closed the gate once again and got up beside Abby, he turned the buggy off the dirt road and through some trees.

"Are we allowed to be here? I hope we're not trespassing or anything." Abby asked a little paranoid.

Levi just laughed and shook his head, "This is my fathers land, so no, and we are not trespassing. I just wanted to share with you the place where I spent most of my childhood play time."

When a small creek came into view, Levi led the horses along side it and up ahead Abby made out a small shack. It was very small, with an actual chimney on its lopsided roof. The walls had an assortment of cracks in it, some large enough to see straight through.

"This is the surprise?" Abby asked with mastered dignity, as she tried not to wrinkle her nose. Levi grinned but said nothing. He stopped the buggy in front of the shack and than got down to open the door for Andrea and the twins. Once they climbed down and started to explore the land, Abby got down from her seat and walked with Levi into the dark hut.

"Stay here a minute while I light a few candles," he advised, carefully walking across the room to the counter underneath an iced up window.

"Why don't I get the basket from the buggy while you set up in here?" Abby proclaimed, turning back to the door.

By the time she came back inside, Levi had set up a blanket on the floor in front of the small fireplace and place candles all around the room, "It looks real cozy in here, Levi."

He smiled up at her from where he knelt in front of the fire, "From the outside it doesn't look like much, but my brother and I made it comfortable on the inside."

It wasn't long before there was a roaring fire in the hearth and the hut became toasty warm. The twins and Andrea came inside than and sat down in front of the fire. "Who wants to hear a story?" Levi asked, settling down beside them as Abby poured some hot chocolate into the tin cups he had provided.

For the rest of the afternoon, they ate from the food Libby had supplied and listened to Levi read from some books he had saved on a desk in the corner. Than, while the three children went outside for a walk, Levi and Abby snuggled up in front of the fire and talked.

"You never told me what was on your mind yesterday. I have never seen you that way before and I kept thinking about it. Is everything okay at work?" she asked, staring at the flames dancing before her.

Sighing, Levi played with a lock of her curly hair, "Something has been bothering me at work, yes. But I don't want to bother you with it; it'll only make you nervous."

Abby turned toward him and looked up into his eyes, "You're scaring me already, so you might as tell me what's on your mind."

"The doctor who I am working under at the hospital is promoting a medication called Miracure, which I happened to find out has only a few different ingredients that might help the common cold. However, he claims that it will help cure many diseases. I had that the lab analyze some tablets for me, but the report was stolen by his helper," he frowned as he spoke, clearly frustrated by the actions of his superior, "I just don't know what to do, Abby."

Abby looked up alarmed, "Did you contact the police? Maybe someone can track them and find out what's going on?"

"I've already talked to the chief of police, Abigail. He said that he can only start an investigation if I have evidence pertaining to the crime."

Voices could be heard from outside and their conversation stopped, but Abby knew that things were about to get scary if Levi would be poking around. She didn't want him to do anything irrational and get into trouble, things were just picking up in their relationship, and she couldn't imagine life without him.

On the way back to the farm, Levi told her to stay in the buggy with the children because it had gotten colder as the night grew near. Abby read to the children by the light of a lantern, but her mind was constantly on him and the situation he was caught in.

Chapter Ten

The following few days were very crazy for her, she spent most of her time in the bookstore. On Tuesday morning, an envelope had come in the mail with the name of a lawyer on the front and Abby had grown too nervous to open it. So, while the children were at school and Esther was in the store, she went to visit her mother. Nothing had prepared her for what she found when she opened the front door of her childhood home though.

Boxes were stacked everywhere and amidst the newspapers and empty boxes in the kitchen stood her mother with dust in her hair. Abby could tell from where she stood at the front door that her mother was tired and nerved up.

"Mom, what's going on?"

Her mother looked up and got up from her haunches, "Hello dear, what are you doing here? Shouldn't you be at the store?"

Abby looked around her room and gestured to the boxes, "I just came to see you, what are all these boxes doing here?"

"Come on in and I'll put on a cup of tea, than we can talk." She turned and moved a box off the counter before plugging in the electric water kettle. Abby took a seat at the table covered in newspapers, and as she pushed them aside, she watched her mother.

"I can't just sit here and wait for you to tell me what's going on,

Mom. Just tell me and get it over with." Abby had enough on her plate and her patience was growing thin.

Her mother went to the fridge and took out a plate of brownies, "Well, alright. But don't start yelling at me, it was my decision."

Once her mother had taken a seat across from her, she started to explain, "Abby, this house is getting too much to handle. It's paid off but I am not making anything anymore, and the little amount of sewing I do barely pays for the groceries."

"Mom, why didn't you tell me? You know I can help you out; I would love too." Abby was surprised to hear what her mother was telling her. She had thought her father had left enough money for her to last at least a few years.

"Honey, what did I just tell you?" she took one of her daughter's hands in her own. "Abby, you have been so good to me. But, this house is just too big to handle. I put it on the market and someone put in an offer. With the money I'll get from this house I can rent a condo in a closed housing facility."

Abby frowned and squeezed her mother's hand, "Are you sure this is what you want?"

Rose nodded solemnly, "Yes honey, I know there are a lot of memories here for you, but it really is getting too much."

The water kettle clicked off than, and she stood up to prepare the tea. As she poured the tea into two mugs, Abby told her about the envelope that had come in the mail that morning.

"Well, aren't you going to open it? If I were you I would have opened it right when I got it; you know how my patience is."

Abby handed it to her mother, "You open it, Mom."

Her eyebrows rose in question but she did as was asked. As she took out the neatly folded papers from the pristine envelope her eyes opened wide and she covered her mouth with her hand, "Oh my."

"What does it say?" Abby shifted nervously in her seat, "Is it bad news?"

"I don't really know what to call it, honey. It says that Andrea's mother wants to give her up for adoption with a real family. She didn't realize you were still unmarried and now she wants what's best for Andrea."

"What?" Abby yelled in anger, "First she sends her daughter away like an unwanted dog, and now she wants to do what's right for her?"

They sat in silence for a while as Abby read the letter herself, and than they decided that she meet with the lawyer, Alex Petri, and talk things over. Than, an idea came to Abby and she grew very excited.

"Mom, what if you didn't have to leave? What if you could live here still and not be alone?"

Her mothers face grew puzzled and she pushed up her horn-rimmed spectacles, "What do you mean, Abby?"

Abby stood up and clapped her hands in excitement, "What if I rent the house from you? The apartment is getting too small for the four of us and I was already thinking about renting a house near the store. This house would be perfect, Mom. There are five bedrooms, which means that the children could each have their own room and you could keep yours."

Her mother sighed and than a small smile came across her lips, "It would be nice to stay here. And if you move in, I could see the twins all the time and improve my relationship with Andrea."

"So, what do you say?" Abby clasped her hands in front of her, dancing on her toes, "Can we unpack?"

"Alright," her mother responded, standing up and hugging her daughter tight, "I would love you to move back in, Abby."

Excited about the news, Abby called Levi to tell him the news. He was just as excited as she was and told her he would come and help her unpack her mother's things. After they hung up, Abby got about unpacking the boxes in the kitchen while her mother phoned the realtor.

As she was down on her knees opening the third box, Abby heard the low rumble of Levi's truck in the drive and ran to greet him at the door. Levi looked freshly showered and very handsome as he bent to kiss her on the cheek. He was dressed in dark blue jeans and a red and white cotton golf shirt.

"Hello gorgeous," he exclaimed, giving her a hug, "You look so happy."

Abby smiled up at him and nodded, "That's because I am. I just don't understand why you call me gorgeous at a time like this. My hair is in every direction and my clothes are all rumpled."

He laughed huskily, the laugh that Abby always enjoyed to listen to," Abby, you look more beautiful than I have ever seen you. Every time I see you I find you more gorgeous than the last time."

Shaking her head at his compliment, Abby pulled him along to the kitchen and together they started setting things back in the cupboards. As they worked side by side on the floor, she told him about the letter that had come in the mail. He was just as shocked as she was about Andrea's mother and he told her that he would go along with her to see the lawyer.

It was near lunchtime and Abby realized that she had to get back to the store so Esther could have her break. Levi volunteered to stay and help her mom with the unpacking. When she got back to the store, Esther was helping an elderly man at the counter and Abby waited until she finished before telling her the news.

"That's wonderful, Abby," she exclaimed, "but I am afraid that I must tell you some bad news."

Abby sat down on the three-legged stool behind the counter, "Okay, what has happened."

Tears came to Esther's eyes as she spoke, "The brethren have decided that I should not work here with an Englisher. One in our community has kindly let me use a room in their loft for our quilting bees. I am very sorry that this does not work out."

This, indeed, was bad news. However, Abby just patted the distraught women on the shoulder and advised her to do as the brethren asked. After Esther left for home, Abby leaned on the counter and prayed silently.

"O almighty God in Heaven. Give me strength and courage to continue in this world. So much has happened in the last while and I am afraid. Be with Levi at work and guide him on a safer way, for only thou knowest what is best. I thank thee for the blessings this day has brought, and for the bad news give me strength to do what is right. Amen."

When Abby looked up after her prayer, she noticed a young woman standing at a rack of books. She was dressed immaculately in a dark blue business suit, which consisted of a long skirt and jacket. Her blonde hair was up in a twist and she wore glasses, which she pushed up on her nose.

"Hello," Abby greeted in a friendly manner, "How are things going?"

The woman looked up and smiled nervously, "Fine, thank you."

Abby took the tone of her voice as a means for no conversation, so she sat back and opened a novel she had been meaning to read. It was a few minutes later before her customer came up to the counter with a few books.

As she rung in the items, the woman asked hesitantly, "I was wondering, do you know of any places that are for rent? My friend and I are looking for a new place."

"Actually I'm going to be moving out of my apartment soon, and I'll be renting that out."

"Really?"

Once she had accepted the twenty-dollar bill from the girl, she handed her the receipt and change, "Yes, I actually just figured this out this morning, and I have some things to work through first. But, I think I'll be out by the end of this month."

"Can I leave my name and number? I would really like to see the apartment if you are sure about renting it out," she questioned excitedly.

Abby provided her with a piece of paper to right her name and number down on, "My name is Abigail Forrester, and I own this bookstore. I'm looking for someone to work for me before I can actually start the moving process, so if you know anyone just let me know, okay?"

"My name is Meredith Green and the girl I'll be living with is Olivia Sanders," she explained, "I am really interested in your home, so please call."

"I will," Abby promised with a smile. Things were really looking up now, she already had someone interested in her place, and she hadn't even advertised. Now, all she needed was someone to work in the store.

That night, over a dinner of mashed potatoes, chicken and cauliflower, Abby told the children about moving to the big house. The twins were excited, but Andrea was upset. She had just finished decorating her room and was content with the room she had. However,

Abby told them that the twins would get their own too, and Andrea could have the attic room, which was twice the size of the room she had now. Andrea than started to warm up to the idea, and even asked questions about how she could decorate the room.

Later, after the twins were tucked in bed, Abby asked Andrea to sit with her in the living room to talk. She was nervous about telling her the bad news, but Andrea had to know what was going on.

"Andrea," she started, "I know that things have been really hard these last few months, but you have adjusted very well. I love you and I would love it if you could stay here."

"Do I hear a but coming, don't I?" Andrea smartly commented, scrunching up her pretty nose.

Abby sighed and than took her hands in her own, "Yes. Your mother's lawyer sent a letter which states that she wants to put you up for adoption."

"Adoption?" Andrea screeched fumingly, "She's my mother! It was bad enough that I had to come here, but now she wants me to live with some people I don't know and call them mom and dad?"

"I know this is hard to believe, honey. If you agree, I would like to adopt you myself. This is going to be really difficult to do because I don't have a husband, but I love you and I want you to be my daughter."

Andrea started to cry hysterically, "I love you too, Abby."

Abby hugged her close, and than asked, "Would you like to be my daughter?"

"Yes," she exclaimed without hesitation.

For the rest of the evening, Abby and Andrea talked about the move to the new house. Andrea had great ideas on how to redecorate the rooms to make them modern, and soon they had vivid sketches to use.

"Are you sure Grandma will let us redecorate? I mean, it is still her house and all…" Andrea asked leaning her head on her hand.

Abby took a sip of her chamomile tea and than sighed, "Well, we did have a lot of memories in that house. I told her that we could leave it but she said that the memories were in the rooms, not the walls."

"Good," Andrea exclaimed, clapping her hands, "I can't wait to redecorate the new house. I have money saved up yet; can I use it to buy some different furniture? There's a writing desk and an easel for sale at the Amish Furniture Auction."

"I don't mind at all, but first; where did you get the money from?"

She blushed, "I'm sorry I didn't tell you, but back with my mom I had babysitting jobs. I was saving that money so I could run away. But, when she decided that I had to leave, she paid. So, now I have a few hundred dollars left over."

"And you haven't used it yet?" Abby amazed, a normal teenaged girl would have spent it at the mall the first chance she got.

Andrea got up from her seat, "I'll be right back."

As she waited for Andrea to return, Abby phoned Levi to see how everything was going. He explained that he had helped until suppertime, ate with her mother and than went to work. Since he wasn't on break, he had to go off the phone, but he told her that he would call when he got the chance.

"Okay," Andrea exclaimed as she came into the room, "You were asking how I never used the money? Here you go."

She handed a small metal box with a tiny slot on the top. The edges were completely welded shut and there was no lock or anything on it.

Grimacing, Andrea sat back down beside Abby and said, "I intended to break it before I left, but that time came when I had not planned. So, I was stuck with a box that couldn't be opened."

"How did you expect to open it?"

"A friend of mine, Jerrod, has Trades in the afternoon at school. He said he would open it for me when I needed it."

Abby shook her head, "Oh boy. Well, at least you found a good way of not spending it."

They laughed together than, and Abby decided to ask Levi to open it for her. Than Andrea headed off for bed and Abby stayed up with a book to wait for Levi's call. However, as she lay down on the couch to wait, she felt herself get tired and it wasn't long before she fell asleep.

Chapter Eleven

Levi hefted his duffle bag off the bed and grabbed the truck keys off the dresser before heading through the kitchen to the front door. He couldn't believe what he was about to do, but he had no choice about the situation. Last night, as he was working in the clinic, he found a piece of paper in the locker room with the name of the Health Officials meeting. Obviously, they were going to try to promote the medication to them at this meeting and by the scrawl of the handwriting, Levi could easily depict it was Larry's.

As he was locking the front door behind him, he heard the sound of a vehicle pulling up in the drive. Groaning in frustration, he turned just in time to see Abby running toward him in angry strides.

"Abby, what are you doing here?" he asked innocently, as he opened the truck door.

Abby's eyes flared, "What are you doing, Levi? I waited all night for you to call me and when you didn't I called the receptionist who told me that you were going away for a while."

Levi sighed and turned towards her, putting his hands up in his defense, "Listen, I am sorry that I didn't tell you about this, but this is important."

"Are you going to tell me about it?" she asked, crossing her arms by her waist.

"Hop in the truck, its warmer in there and I'll tell you everything." Levi replied, giving in.

She complied and as Levi turned the truck on, she asked, "Did something happen in your family?"

"No," he sat back and turned his body towards her, "I'm just going to a Health Society meeting. I'll be back in a few days."

Abby frowned, "A Health Society meeting; are you even allowed to be there?"

He shook his head, "Nope, but I need to go there because I heard that Dr. Larry is going to be there and I need to speak before he does."

"You can't go there, Levi. These guys are dangerous, you have to let the law handle this." Abby looked like she might cry, and Levi took her shaking hands in his and squeezed them.

"But I am the only one who knows about the contents of the medicine, Abby. I need more evidence before the police will do anything."

A lone tear went down Abby's cheek and Levi reached up to catch it as she spoke, "Well, than I'm coming with you. I won't let you go alone."

Levi slammed his fist against the steering wheel, "No, you're staying here. I don't want you to be in any danger."

"If I don't go, than you don't either. I'll phone my mom and she can take the kids for a few days, it'll be okay." Abby took his hands in hers once again, "We just have to pray that everything will be okay."

"Alright," Levi agreed quietly, "Okay, why don't we stop in at your place and you can pack up some clothes before we go, and call your mother, jah."

Abby smiled than and hugged him close, "Thank you Levi, this means so much to me."

Levi released her slowly, "At least I have someone to talk to on the way. It's a few hours drive from here, so it can get quite boring after a long while."

It wasn't much longer before they pulled into a parking spot in front of the Bookworm, and Levi waited in the store while Abby ran upstairs to pack. He leafed through some books, and he was just placing a book back on the shelf, when a knock sounded on the front door.

A young woman dressed in a business suit stood at the door entrance peering through the window. The store was closed up, so it surprised him that she was waiting for someone to come and answer her knock.

He strode over to the double doors and opened it slightly, "Hello, is there anything I can help you with?"

"Yes," she exclaimed, "I am looking for the owner? I told her I was interested in renting the apartment from her, and my friend and I have to be out of our place by next week, so we were wondering if there is any chance of moving in by than."

Levi sighed, "Well, it might take a little longer than that, but there is a boarding house up the street where you could stay for a while. Abby and I are going to be out of town for a few days on business, but when we return we'll be all about moving."

The young woman smiled than and thanked him. Just as he was closing the door one again, Abby came down the back stairs with a small suitcase in one hand and her purse and keys in another, "Who was at the door?"

"That was the woman who wants to rent the room from you. She says she's ready to move in already because they have to be out of their other place by next week."

She put down the suitcase at the counter and picked up the phone, "Alright. I hope you told her that we'll be gone a few days."

"Jah, I did. And I also told her that the boarding house up the street would be a good place to stay awhile."

Abby nodded, and than punched in a set of numbers on the phone, "I'm just going to phone my mother a minute."

While she spoke to her mother, Levi carried her luggage to the truck and than walked to the gas station up the street to buy some snacks for the trip. When he returned with a bag full of goodies, Abby was just locking up.

"My mother will pick up the twins from school, and I phoned Andrea's school to let them know that she has to be dropped off at my mothers."

They got into the truck and Levi maneuvered the truck back on the road, leading up to the I-90. The trip up to Landenberg was seven hours, and since it was nearing ten o'clock, it meant that they would be there at about five. The meeting was scheduled for seven, so that gave them enough time to check into a motel for the night and have a decent dinner.

During the drive up, Abby and Levi kept a light conversation going. It wasn't long however, before Abby dropped off to sleep, her head nestled up against his shoulder. Levi looked down at her dark curls cascading around her face; she was so beautiful. He was angry with himself for letting her come along. She shouldn't be with him right now, when she could be at home with the kids, safe.

The town of Landenberg wasn't as small as Levi had first anticipated. When they turned off the I-90 and headed in the direction of the Health Officials Building, he noticed by the lights of the town, that it went for miles across.

"Hey, Abby," he exclaimed, gently nudging her awake, "We're here." Abby had dosed off and on during the trip, clearly tired from not getting enough sleep the night before.

Abby stretched and yawned at the same as he pointed in the direction they were going. They both had no idea what the night had in store for them, but they were anxious to get out of the truck and walk off the cramps that were setting in. Levi could barely feel his legs any more because about half way the trip the heater quit in the truck. He had given the only blankets he had for Abby to snuggle in, and now his legs felt like lead.

They pulled off the road and down a main two-lane street, "Do you want to eat first or book in."

Shrugging, Abby yawned again and replied, "Why don't we book in first; that way we don't have to rush through dinner."

Levi decided that it was a good idea, and they drove through the town looking for a good motel. About five minutes down the street, Abby pointed out a dignified Royal Hotel held back a bit from the busy traffic. They quickly booked in for two rooms beside each other and than both went into their separate rooms to freshen up.

"I don't know if this is a good idea, Levi," Abby exclaimed, a little frightened. They were parked a block from the Health Society Building and Levi was talking her through the events to come. They had eaten at a Denny's restaurant near the Hotel and than went straight across town to the building.

Levi shook his head, "Abby, if you don't feel comfortable with this you should probably just stay in the truck."

"Stay in here and freeze? No, thank you. I'd rather brave your adventure scheme than catch pneumonia or frost bite," she shuddered as she spoke and Levi chuckled at her slight exaggeration.

It wasn't long before they stood in front of the tall building complex. Levi had already located Larry's Beamer out in the parking lot, and was deciding about the best way to go in.

Abby stomped her feet as the bitter cold was attacking her legs; one of the downfalls of skirts, "Let's just go inside, and decide there, I'm freezing."

Levi looked at her with raised eyebrows, as if challenging her to complain more. She knew that he was trying to think so she let him ponder on his decision.

"Okay, I have an idea. Larry doesn't really know you as well as me, jah?"

"Yes," Abby had only met him once at the church, and he had barely glanced her way, "What do you want me to do."

"You go in first and ask the receptionist to call one of the Society members out. Tell her that the information you have for them pertains to the meeting they are having tonight." Levi put a hand on her shoulder and than guided her through the double doors.

They went up the elevator together and when the doors opened, Abby walked ahead of him down the long hallway. When they got to the end the hallway turned left, and Abby peeked around and than leaned back.

"The reception desk is right around the corner. Should I go first and talk to her?"

Levi nodded silently and waited while she calmly walked around the corner. He heard her speak cordially to the receptionist about the weather and then the reason for stopping by. As soon as she said she had information pertinent to the meeting, he heard the receptionist stand up from her chair and walk briskly away.

Abby than came back to him, "She's going to call someone."

"I know," Levi said with a smile, "But go back, or she'll get suspicious."

It was a few minutes before he heard footsteps and voice coming towards them. Quickly, he went around the corner just as Abby was shaking hands with a tall man in his thirties. He wore a blue suit with a red tie and his dark hair was styled neatly.

"I heard you have some information for me about the meeting we're about to have. How did you hear about this?"

Levi introduced himself and was just about to tell him what he had found out when the elevator doors opened and Larry and his 'colleague' stepped out. Larry's face flamed beat red when he saw them standing there, but he walked towards them with a fake smile on his face.

"Hello, Mr. Angelo," he greeted, "Is the meeting about ready to begin?"

Mr. Angelo nodded toward the two men and than asked Levi, "Do you still have anything to say?"

"No,"

"Alright," Mr. Angelo looked at him as if he wasn't sure about it, gestured than towards Larry and his accomplice to lead the way toward the boardroom.

As they passed by Larry put his head close to Levi's, and spoke in a low and assured voice, "If I ever hear that you have been snitching about Miracure, I will come after you."

Abby's face was pale as they rode the elevator down, and Levi pulled her into his embrace and kissed the top of her head, "It's all right, we'll get them some other way."

Back down in the parking lot, Levi noticed that his truck seemed lower to the ground than normal. Instinct kicked in and he ran to his vehicle to check the tires, "They cut the tires, Abby. They're all flat; right down the ground."

"Oh, this is nuts," Abby ran a hand through her hair and walked over to where he stood, "What are we going to do?"

"Well, we can't phone Sean because he doesn't know we're down here. I assume we must call a tow truck and than take a taxi back to the motel to wait till the tires are fixed."

Levi heard a knock on his door around six thirty and opened it to find Abby on the other side, smiling. She wore her hair up in a twist with soft curls framing her face. And the red dress she wore made his heart beat twice as fast as it normally did around her.

"Well, you are sure a surprise!" he said, stretching his arms out in emphasis, "You look wonderful-gut!"

"I made dinner in my motel room and if you hurry and change you can see what I made!" she said with a smile, "Maybe we can forget about all the worries for a little while."

Laughing, Levi kissed her gently and told her to head back to her room and he would meet her in fifteen minutes. As soon as she closed, the door behind her Levi went to his suitcase and pulled out a pair of gray slacks and a crisp white button down shirt. He wondered how Abby had gotten the dress and the groceries. They had decided to take a nap before dinner because they hadn't gotten enough overnight.

Levi took a quick shower and than headed over to Abby in the next room. When he walked into the room, he noticed that there were candles all over and a table was set up in between the two double beds. She had put a set of candles on the table and some red wine, along with rose peddles.

"You did all this?"

"Yes, I wanted it to be special for us. Do you like it?"

Levi took her in his arms and hugged her tight, "You are so wonderful Abby, and this is just what we both needed. How did you get this all together?"

She went over to the small counter in the kitchen area and brought over two small bowls of salad, "This afternoon I walked over the grocery store and than I went to a thrift store and found this beautiful dress."

"Denki, Abby."

They prayed for their food and Levi asked for protection and safety. He was feeling scared ever since they found the tires slashed; he now knew what those men were capable of.

As they ate the delicious meal Abby had prepared, they talked about Andrea and how she wanted to be a part of the family. Levi was very happy that she had asked Abby to be her mom; she needed a family and had come a long way since her first day in town. When he had first met her, she wasn't very talkative, but every time he saw her after that, she became more out going and fun.

Once their dinner finished and Levi had read a portion out of the Bible and prayed, they both washed the dishes and than sat down on one of the beds and talked.

"What did you want to be when you were younger?" Levi asked her, putting an arm around her shoulders and drawing her close.

Abby laced her fingers through his hand on her shoulder, "A marine biologist. My Dad took us to the local aquarium every summer and I absolutely loved it. It was always such a special place to be with him because he knew so much about marine life."

Sighing, Levi said with a quiet voice, "The only special memories I had with my Dat were working side by side in the field. As a family we didn't go on any trips, but we did have community outings: barn raises, picnics and things like that."

"Everyone has different aspects of special memories, Levi. When I was young I hardly seen my father, he was always gone in the Navy. However, during the summer when he was on leave we spent everyday together. The Navy and computers had always fascinated Mike, so he combined them in his work. You were lucky to have your father home all year long."

"I guess I was, but he's a very hard man to understand. I still have that cigar box in the truck, you know." Levi grunted and shook his head, "My Dat was so angry when we left that I am so scared of what he will say. I have seen him at Abe's but he has never spoken to me or paid me any attention."

Abby turned and looked up into his eyes, "I'll go with you when we get home, okay?"

Levi shook his head, "No, I think I should do this on my own."

"If you do this on your own, you never will get up the courage to go. I am going with you and that's the end of this discussion." Abby gave him a quick kiss and than stood up from the bed, "I think it is time you go to your room now, Levi."

He nodded and slid off the bed, "Jah, I should."

Abby walked him to the door and he enveloped her in a tight hug, "I love you, Abby."

She froze for a moment and than kissed him but said nothing. When he got back to his room, he wondered why she had not responded in the same. Did she love him back? Or was it too soon to tell? Groaning, he undid his tie and threw it over the chair; he would just have to wait.

Chapter Twelve

The next morning, fog had enveloped the motel and as he walked toward the Ernie's Tire Shop, Levi could barely see ahead of him. He had left Abby at the motel to do some research on one of the available computers in the lobby. The tire shop was one block from the motel so it wasn't too long of a walk. Ernie sat outside on a chair drinking from a large coffee cup, and when he spotted Levi, walking up he stood up on wobbly legs and walked into the shop with him.

"We put four new tires on for ya," Ernie exclaimed, walking over to the raised truck, "The tires were very badly slashed, sir. You better talk to the police about it."

Levi nodded absently and watched as the old man pushed a button to get the truck down. He didn't feel right loading all his problems on the man's shoulders, so he just let it slide and followed him into the office.

"That'll come to four hundred and fifty three dollars, sir." Ernie announced, handing him a bill.

As Levi wrote out a check, Ernie said a cheerful hello to a young worker who came in and went into the back room, "How many men do you have working for you?" he asked.

"Two right now, but my grandson is graduating soon and than he'll be working for me as well."

Levi took the keys from Ernie and smiled, "Denki for getting the truck done so quickly."

"Oh, it was no problem, sir."

They said goodbye and than Levi headed back to the motel, where Abby was ready to go. After packing up their luggage, they headed to a service station to tank up on gas. Abby went inside and bought some juice and granola bars for the trip back. Than she used the pay phone to call her mother and see how the children were doing. From the sound of things, the twins were just rascally as ever. And Andrea was already busy in her attic bedroom.

Levi was in a goofy mood and he had Abby laughing for the first few hours of the trip. Than he put on a tape of hymns and they sang together, just enjoying each other's company. He still wondered if she had wanted to respond to his exclamation of his love for her or if she just wasn't ready. Deciding he wouldn't pressure her into anything, he settled back in his seat and told himself to relax.

An hour later, Abby pointed out a sign that indicated a hiking trail up ahead and asked if he wanted to get out and stretch his legs. Eagerly, he turned off onto a gravel road that took them up to a long parking lot filled with vehicles.

"Sure looks busy here, it must be a nice walk." Levi exclaimed, parking his truck between two cars.

Abby put the juice bottles and a few granola bars in her shoulder bag and stepped out, "It's been a while since I went for a walk down a nature trail."

They set off down the narrow trail leading through a thick forest hand in hand, greeting passersby with a friendly hello. By the time they returned to the truck an hour later, they were refreshed and happy from the walk.

During the rest of the trip, Levi let Abby drive back. He lay down with his coat behind his head, and listened to her sing in that soft voice along with the hymns.

"Come thou fount of every blessing
Tune my heart to sing Thy grace
Streams of mercy, never ceasing
Call for songs of loudest praise
Teach me some melodious sonnet

94

Sung by flaming tongues above
Praise the mount-I'm fixed upon it
Mount of Thy redeeming love."

"You have an amazing voice, darlin'," he exclaimed, smiling up at her from where he sat, "I love to hear you sing. You should join the church choir."

Abby blushed, "Thanks for the compliment, but I don't think I would have the time to join in the choir."

"You should just make time; Andrea is old enough to baby-sit and once you're moved in you're mom's house you'll have some free nights."

"I never really thought about that, but that does sound nice. Maybe you could join too, you have a good voice you know," she advised, smiling in his direction for second.

The fog had lifted at about three o'clock, and they were both ready to be back at home. Although the trip had turned out better than both of them had first anticipated, they were ready to get back to their regular lives. Abby told him that she was eager to move into her mother's house and become settled there. She knew that the move was going to be very time-consuming, so she wanted to get started on it right away. Levi promised her that he would get Mike and Pete together to help with the loading and unloading, so that would take a lot of worry off her shoulders.

When they finally got back to Churchville, Abby drove straight to her mother's house to pick up the children. Levi could tell that she was anxious to see them; she had told him earlier that she had never left the children overnight for a long time, except to stay at her ex-in-laws.

As they drove down Avalon Street towards the large Victorian house, Abby and Levi gasped at the sight of two ambulances in front of the house and a police car, "What's goin' on?" Levi asked in a panic.

They parked the car on the opposite side of the street and ran across to talk to anyone who might explain what had happened. Through the crowd, Levi spotted Sean talking to a few Paramedics and pulled Abby along with him to their side.

"Sean," Levi barked in exasperation, "What is goin' on around here? What happened?"

Sean looked at them both with sorrowful eyes, "You better come with me inside the neighbor's home and sit down; there is no good way for me to tell you the news."

Levi held up Abby's limp body and walked beside her into the house, where a young woman with tears in her eyes led them to the living area. Once they were seated on the loveseat hand in hand, Sean took a seat across from them on the sofa.

"First, I want to tell you as your friend how truly sorry I am to be the bearer of such news." Sean said as tears streamed down his face, "There's been a fire in your mother's room over night. Someone through a beer bottle filled with gasoline in the room and than something to light it, probably a match box or a lighter."

Abby started to cry as she asked in a wobbly voice, "And my mother, how is she?"

Sean wiped the tears from his face and uncomfortably shifted in his seat, "I'm sorry Abby, she didn't survive the fire."

"And the children?" Levi asked, putting his arm around Abby to comfort her, "Are they alright?"

"They are all in the hospital being looked over. Andrea is the worst of them all, she hurt her leg, succumbed to smoke inhalation, and her lungs are swollen from being stuck up in the attic. She'll be staying in for a few days so they can monitor her. The twins both suffered smoke inhalation and are traumatized, but they will be allowed to go home tomorrow."

Abby grasped Levi's shirt in her hands and said firmly, "You have to take me to them right now, Levi. I need to see them."

Levi nodded without saying a word and than thanked Sean for being there for them. Since they were both too worked up to drive, Levi allowed Sean to drive them to the hospital in his cruiser.

All three of the injured children were sleeping soundly when they got to their room. The kind doctor had allowed them all to be in the same private room so they wouldn't be scared. He assured them that they were doing much better, and that Andrea had been given some pain medication a while ago, so she could sleep. But, Abby had a hard time understanding the words the doctor spoke, for her heart was in too much pain. She ran over to each bed and kissed them on the cheek. When she got to Andrea's bed and saw the paleness of her face and the dark circles around her eyes she screamed out in pain and than sobbed all over the blanket.

Levi went up behind her and put his hands on her shoulders unsure of what to do. She was so broken up, first her mother had passed away, and than her children were all hospitalized, it was all too much to handle at once.

"What am I going to do, Levi? What am I going to do without my mother?" she cried out in desperation falling weakly into his arms.

Unable to voice the words resounding in his heart, he just held her close and kissed her neck. She just sobbed onto his shoulder and he whispered soothing words in her ear. Than when they both regained enough strength, they sat down on the little bench in the corner of the room and prayed.

It was nearly midnight before Levi pulled up a comforter over Abby who was fast asleep on the hospital cot. She hadn't wanted to leave the children, so Levi had asked a nurse for a cot. However, it was a long time before Abby fell asleep; she had too much on her mind and even Levi couldn't put her mind at ease. They had to finally result to a sleeping pill, which Abby had protested against fully. Levi headed over to the phone in the hall to call Sean. He knew that he was still awake because he was at the station going over the facts of the fire.

"Hey Levi, how are you holding up?" Sean asked with worry on his voice when he answered the phone.

Tears came to Levi's eyes as he spoke, "I don't know what to do anymore, I feel so useless seein' Abby with so much hurt in her eyes."

Sighing deeply as if concentrating on the right words to say, Sean replied briskly, "Levi, I cannot imagine what you are going through right now; but what you should know is that you can always pray to God for help. He hears you always."

Suddenly, all of the pain trapped in his heart came free and he sobbed in deep wretches. The receiver he held in his hand fell down on its cord and he sank to his knees in weakness. Everything that had happened was just too much for him to handle; he did not know how he was going to comfort Abby and himself at the same time.

A soft tap on his shoulder made him shift to look at the person behind the hand, and found a young nurse looking down at him with worry on her face, "Are you okay, sir?"

"Nah, but I just need some time to collect myself," he admitted, struggling to his weary feet, "I'm just having a hard time overcoming all that has happened today."

She pointed in the direction of a waiting room, "You can rest in there if you want, I'll close the door, and you can have the room to yourself. There aren't many people here this late anyway."

Levi thanked her and picked himself up from the floor. The nurse brought him a blanket and pillow and than closed the door behind him, allowing him to rest alone.

The next morning, Levi woke to the sounds of people bustling around outside the waiting room. Yawning, he sat upright on the couch and rubbed the sleepers from his eyes. Thoughts of the night before came to mind and he jumped up suddenly alert. When he got to the right room, he found Abby sleeping beside Chloe on the hospital bed. Her dark curls framed her face and spread across the pillow beside her, she looked so peaceful and calm. He stood at the end of the bed just watching her, but it wasn't long before her eyelashes started to flutter and she caught him gazing at her.

"Good morning beautiful," he said with a smile, "How are you holding up?"

She yawned and covered her mouth with the back of her hand and than sat up slowly, "I slept."

He came to her and took her hand in his, "I see that, but I thought you were sleeping on the cot."

"Chloe started screaming early this morning so I crawled in with her," she looked up at him with tears brimming in her eyes, "We really have to talk, Levi; but we can't talk in here."

"Come on," he exclaimed, "Let's go to the cafeteria and get something to eat and than you can tell what is troubling you."

There weren't too many people in the large cool room, and after they filled their plates at the buffet, they took a seat near the back.

Levi prayed softly out loud holding her hands in his, *"Our Father which art in Heaven, hallowed be thy name, Thy kingdom come, Thy will be done on earth as it is in Heaven. Give us this day our daily bread and forgive us our debts as we forgive our debtors. Lead us not into temptation but deliver us from evil, for Thine is the kingdom, the power and the glory. Amen."*

They ate silently for a while, but Levi could tell that Abby was nervous about something and he couldn't bare seeing her so uncomfortable with him, "What did you want to talk about."

Abby pushed her half-filled plate away and clasped her hands together on the table, "I don't know any other way to say what I have to so I'm just going to come out and say it."

"Alright," Levi put his fork down to listen attentively to what she had to say.

"I don't think we should see each other anymore. I don't want anything else bad to happen to the children. Everything has just been so scary since I have been with you," tears spilled from her eyes as she spoke and her voice was warbled, "I really do love you Levi, but I don't think I can bare any more of the danger."

Levi clasped her hands in his own as tears come to his eyes as well, "I know that this has been very scary for all of us and I am so sorry about your mother, Abby. But, do we really have to stop being friends forever?"

"Not if everything gets settled and you're life gets back to normal. I think it would be best if we just stopped seeing each other for a while." The words she spoke were interrupted with sobs and she laid her head down on their clasped hands. Levi swallowed back tears, trying to be strong for her. He didn't want their relationship to end, but he also did not want any more danger to come to them. He hugged her close and than kissed her forehead, "I don't want anything else to happen to you either. Can you at least let me help fixing the house?"

"If that's what you want," she replied curtly, slowly pushing him away. He could instantly tell how much this was hurting her, and so he moved far from her in order to save her the pain.

The funeral service for Abby's mother was that afternoon, and through out the whole ordeal Levi noticed how distracted Abby was. She was probably upset that the children couldn't be there. Mike stood beside her on one side and him on the other at the graveside and than Mike read a passage from the Bible.

"In Isaiah fifty-seven versus one and two, we read: *'The righteous perisheth, and no man layeth it to heart: and merciful men are taken away, none considering that the righteous is taken from the evil to come. He shall enter into peace: they shall rest in their beds, each one walking in his uprightness.'* Our mother was a strong woman who had a kind and generous heart, but we do not know if God cleansed her heart, for only He can know that. However, we stand here today to mourn her loss and keep the memory of her faithfulness in life and love in our hearts."

As Mike spoke, Levi glanced at Abby who now had her hand over her face to hide the pain expressed there. He wanted to take her into his arms and comfort her, but after the words she had said before, he was unsure of her response. It was going to be a long day.

When Levi got home to rest after the funeral, he could not sleep. So he called Todd to arrange the reconstruction of the house, and they decided to start the next day. Levi stayed up all night writing a list of things that needed to be done at the house, and he even drove out to the house to make sure he hadn't missed anything. Than, as soon as the sun peeked out over the horizon, he phoned to get a large garbage bin brought over and than started working.

He was just carrying out the last burnt furnishings from the master bedroom when a large van pulled into the driveway and out piled half dozen men. Right behind them came Todd's work truck and another van. Surprised, Levi dropped the desk beside the bin and walked over to Todd, saying hello to the men talking together in the driveway.

"Hello, Levi, I brought a few extra hands to help get this place in order. I hope you don't mind." He stood with a wide grin on his face as he gestured toward those behind him.

Levi chuckled softly, "Not at all, denki."

After producing his list from his pocket, Todd divided it amongst the men, and soon the sounds of pounding hammers, loud footsteps and laughter could be heard all around the site. Levi and Todd went into town, living Mike (who had come just as they were leaving) in charge. Todd spent his own money on new plywood and insulation, while Levi bought paint for the house and other needed supplies, such as cleaning supplies and fans for in the windows.

As they stood at the counter paying for the supplies, a young police officer got a call on his radio as he stood behind them. A voice announced that there had been a car accident and they were in need of more assistance. A woman in a red Bronco was in a bad situation.

Levi was talking to the cashier while this was going on, but Todd had heard it all, "Levi, what kind of vehicle does Abby drive?" he asked, nudging him with his elbow as Levi put his wallet back in his pocket.

Immediately his face grew pale and he nodded, "What happened?" he asked looking behind at the police officer.

Todd pointed to the police officer and Levi charged over to him, "What just happened? Please tell me what you just heard."

The gruff man backed away, obviously insulted by the forward man charging at him, "Hands off, sir. I can't help you when you come at me like that."

Relaxing his form just a little, Levi stepped back and than spoke in still a frantic voice, "A friend of mine drives a Bronco and I need to know what just happened."

The man tilted his cap back and switched his gaze between the two men, "Well I only know that a serious accident happened involving a '92 Bronco. I'm heading over to the scene right now if you want to catch a ride."

"Jah, I will come along." Levi exclaimed right away, "Todd, can you handle everything?"

His blonde haired friend assured him that it was all right and than Levi went out to the cruise with Officer Adams and soon they were racing toward the scene with the lights flashing.

Levi's stomach did somersaults as they arrived at the site. His eyes flashed to the vehicle on the rocks below the bridge. It was completely smashed in and Levi ran down the narrow slope to the vehicle, but was pulled back by an officer who pointed to two men with a saw. Levi looked at the drivers' side and saw a dark brown lock of curly hair; instantly he fell to his knees in the mud and prayed as sobs wretched from his weak body. He asked God to give him strength and Abby the courage to pull through.

A hand touched his shoulder and he looked up into the grey eyes of his good friend Pete, "Levi, I heard the call from the hospital and caught a ride with a friend. What's going on?"

Wiping the tears from his eyes, Levi stood up and shook his head in utter disbelief, "I don't know Pete, I am just too scared to ask. They're going to take her out with the Jaws of Life, so it must be bad, jah?"

Pete gave his friend a comforting hug and said, "I'll just go and ask the paramedics. Why don't you sit on those rocks," he pointed in the direction of the side of the river, "You'll do better by letting the people get her out safely."

"I just can't believe it," he exclaimed as Pete walked with him over debris, "I feel like I'm destroying her life. This must have something to do with Larry and his friends, jah?"

"I think so, but we should talk to the police and get all the facts first. Why don't I go talk to a few people and see what's going on?" He waited until Levi found a comfortable spot on the rough rocks, and than went back up the slope to the array of cars above.

Levi tried to relax a little on the rocks alongside the rivers bank, but his stomach kept churning and his head was pounding something fierce. He watched as the paramedics sawed through the rubble in order to pull Abby out and tears started to form in his eyes again. He had been taught since childhood to forgive those who wronged him, but now he only felt anger and hatred toward Larry and his cohorts. Inside he knew that it was they who had caused the accident. But why were they going to such lengths to protect the medicine?

It was another half hour before they were able to get Abby out safely and onto the stretcher. While Levi had waited, Pete came to tell him the news from the paramedics and police. Abby's legs had been severely caught under the steering wheel and she had smashed her head on the driver's side window so she was unconscious. They had little hope for saving her legs. The police informed Pete that she had not been hit because no other vehicle was involved. He immediately phoned Sean who said he would investigate the vehicles parts to see if anything had been tampered with.

When Abby was placed in the ambulance, Levi was allowed to go with the paramedics in the back. He was comforted with the notion that Pete and Sean were doing their best to uncover the truth behind the accident. One of the paramedics gave him his cell phone to call Mike and ask him to pick up the twins who were being released from the hospital. He immediately asked how Abby was doing and than said, he would pick up the twins and bring them over to his flat.

Once at the hospital, Abby was carried away on the stretcher with doctors and nurses bellowing out commands back and forth, as they went down the long hallway. Levi stood in the Emergency entrance shaking and alone. A dark friendly man walked over and led him to a private waiting area where he brought him some coffee.

"As soon as I can I'll ask how things are progressing in the OR. If you have any questions, my name is James so just ask at the front desk."

In a complete daze, Levi watched him walk away and than rested his head on the back on the couch as held the hot cup of coffee between his fingers.

Chapter Thirteen

A low beeping sounded when Abby came to. Where was she? She opened her eyes and found herself lying in a bed staring up at a white ceiling. The room she was in had bright lights and an airy feeling; all around her unfamiliar sounds drifted towards her. Hoses were connected to her nose and others to her arms. Groaning, she tried to move her legs to get more comfortable, but nothing happened. Frustrated she tried again, and still nothing happened.

Beside her on a chair, a man slept with his head on his shoulder. Abby watched him as he breathed in and out and whistled slightly through his mouth. His tanned face was intriguing and her heart leapt at the curls splayed out over his forehead. Who was this handsome man?

"Who...who..." she croaked, than cleared her throat and tried again; by that time he was up and by her bed, "Who...are...you?"

He smiled, his deep chocolate eyes filled with tears, "Abby, you're awake! I'm Levi, your boyfriend, don't you remember?"

A frown crossed her pale face, "Where's Charlie?"

Levi paled and looked away from her a moment before returning to her face, "Oh honey, you don't remember anything?"

"Where's Charlie, I want to talk to my fiancé."

"Your fiancé?"

"Yes," looked angry now, "My fiancé!"

Levi started to cry silently and sagged back into the chair by the bedside. Suddenly big burst of sobs erupted from his body.

"If you're my boyfriend, what happened to Charlie?" she asked, trying to sit up.

A nurse in bright pink scrubs came in that and told Levi to leave while she checked the bandages.

Levi left as the nurse pulled the blankets back. Abby gasped in horror sight and shouted out in anger, "What have you done to my legs?"

The small nurse jumped back in alarm, "Calm down, ma'am, the doctor will explain everything in a few minutes."

"Calm down?" she screamed, flinging her arm at the young bewildered nurse, "Calm down? My legs are gone, how can I calm down? How will I walk down the aisle on my wedding day without legs?"

Just than an elderly man in a long white straight jacket came into the room and motioned for the nurse to leave.

"Are you my doctor?" Abby asked loudly still glaring slightly in the direction of the frazzled nurse.

He bobbed his head as he sat in a chair at the bedside, "Yes, I am Doctor Metford."

"Good," she muttered anxiously, "Perhaps you can explain to me how my legs disappeared and how a strange man is telling me I'm his girlfriend when I already am engaged to someone else."

The doctor sighed, pushed his glasses higher up on his arched nose and opened the file on his clipboard, "Let's see, your name is Abigail Forrester, you are a widow with two twins, and you're a guardian over a fourteen year old girl. You own a bookstore called the Bookworm, which you inherited from your grandfather…"

"Hold on," Abby retorted, holding up a hand, "I'm a widow? Charlie died?"

"That's correct, ma'am."

She started to cry, "What happened? Just tell me what happened please."

"Someone either drove you off a bridge or tampered with your car. You are involved with Levi and he's been having trouble with some men who are selling a drug called Miracure. Levi has reason to believe this drug is a hoax, and these men don't want him to release this information. They knew you two were involved and somehow caused you to have the accident. You were on your way to pick up the children from the hospital; they were recently in a house fire."

"House fire?" she asked quietly, "how are they?"

"The children are fine, but your mother did not survive."

Abby shuddered, "My mother is gone too? What else has gone wrong?"

"You'll have to talk to Levi about that, dear."

She nodded, "So, you had to take my legs?"

"We couldn't get you out in time and you were loosing too much blood. We had no choice."

"Just send Levi in please. I want to apologize to him."

The battered doctor nodded calmly, "I will. But let me tend to your bandages first."

Levi sat in the waiting room crying. It was his entire fault. He should have never left her alone. Now she had amnesia and she would never be able to walk again.

Across the room, Mike sat with his head in his hands, he had brought the twins to his flat but when he heard how bad it was, he dropped the twins of at their grandparents and came to the hospital. Andrea was still in the hospital but she was sleeping when he last saw her. Her friend Kiera was keeping her company while they waited on results from Abby's doctor. Levi was glad the children were not there to see the state their mother was in.

As the hallway lights blinked on and off slowly, Levi watched as the nurses and doctors scurried in and out of Abigail's room. His watch showed three-thirty am and he didn't feel tired at all.

"Levi," a soft male voice called out, jerking Levi back.

"Jah," Levi mumbled in feigned English, "What is it, Mike?"

Mike stood beside him, a hand comfortably resting on his shoulder, "I'm going to get some coffee; do you want to come with?"

Levi shook his head violently, "Nah, I have to stay here in case she needs me. "

"Alright, should I bring you a cup?"

"Ach, that'd be wonderful-gut Mike, denki."

"After Mike left, Levi felt so lonesome; he wished his family could be there to comfort him and talk to him. A pay phone sat in the corner of the waiting room and Levi went over to call Todd. Todd was very understanding and sympathetic and claimed he would do his best in getting the house wheel chair proof as well.

As he hung up Mike came back with the coffee and just as they were about to sit down; Doctor Medford asked Mike to come in and talk to Abby.

Levi waited nervously in the waiting room and as soon as Mike returned ten minutes later, he jumped up and came to him with questions in his eyes.

Signs of tears formed in Mike's eyes, "She really doesn't remember about Charlie's death; does she?"

Levi held him in a manly yet caring hug and cried with him. He knew the pain he was feeling and wanted to help ease it.

Mike pushed back and wiped the tears from his eyes, but more came in there place, "I suppose you'll only want to friends with Abigail now. There are so many obligations involved in caring for her now."

They each took a seat across from each other, "Of course I still want to be with her, Mike. I love her; I have fallen deeply in love with over these last few months. And I am definitely here for the long haul!"

"Levi?" Dr. Medford called out, as he walked into the private waiting room, "Abby would like to see you before she goes to sleep."

Jumping up, Levi rubbed the tears off his face before heading into the white room. Just as before, Abby lay in the hospital bed looking ashen and disheveled, yet so entirely beautiful. His gaze fell on the empty space halfway down the bed and tears sprung to his eyes again.

"Gut-daag," he said softly as he walked to her bedside.

Abby met his gaze with a slight smile, her eyes heavy from the drugs, "Hello Levi."

"How are you feeling? Is there any more pain?"

"I'm fine," she said curtly, "I asked you to come in so I could apologize for my earlier behavior, I was rude, and I should have listened to you."

"Nah," Levi held up his hand, "You have nothin' to apologize for. If anything, I'm the one at fault for your accident. I should never have let you be alone after all the trouble we've been having."

Abby shook her head, "It wasn't your fault Levi. Even though I don't remember anything about these last few years, it doesn't mean my faith is gone. I have faith in you."

"And God?"

"No." she said curtly, looking away from his gaze.

"You don't have faith in God."

She shook her head and looked back at him with an icy glare, "Why should I? I'm never going to walk again. Charlie's dead and I can't remember why, I have children I can't remember I've had and my mother is dead. Plus, I am dating a complete stranger."

Levi leaned over the bedpost and kissed her lightly on her lips. She sighed and curled her arms around to draw him closer. Than, just like a switch changed and she pushed him away, "Stay away from me, Levi. I don't want to ruin your life."

"Oh Abby," he sighed, "You could never ruin my life. If anything, you've saved it."

"Just leave, Levi."

Levi turned and went to the door and than turned once again, "Take care, love. I'll let you get some rest."

In the waiting room, Levi walked back and forth before storming back into Abby's room.

"I am not leaving you here alone, Abby. I love and I will stay with you through thick and thin. So you lost your legs; you still have a wonderful and generous heart, a gorgeous face and two loving arms. I love you Abby, so you're not getting rid of me that easily." After he got those words off his chest, he wheeled around and left the shocked patient behind to ponder over his words.

Instead of going home and resting as Mike had suggested, Levi first went to Andrea and gave her an update before going to the Forrester's to pick up the twins. After thinking it over, he decided to move into Abby's apartment while the house was being renovated.

The Forrester's lived in Central Heights, the neighborhood of the rich and famous. All the homes were excessively large with pin neat yards, and the Forrester's three-story mansion was no different. The entire front of the home was made of glass, some might call it beautiful, but Levi thought it cold.

He parked his rusty pick-up in front of the wide doors and than waited in the lobby while the butler went in search of the twins and their grandparents. Levi waited patiently, eyeing the modern furniture and art in the library to the left.

"Mr. Bontrager!" a deep baritone boomed from behind Levi as he gazed at a painting of a woman. Levi turned and found himself looking straight into the face of Roger Forrester.

Levi held out his hand for him to shake, "Gut daag, sir. I'm here to pick up the twins."

"Good," he remarked coldly, "They've been terrorizing the place and Gwen and I are going to Italy tomorrow."

"Italy?" Levi retorted in anger, "What about Abby? She needs you right now."

Roger pointed a chubby finger in Levi's face, "Now you listen here, Bontrager, Abigail brought this on herself. None of this would have happened if she hadn't started seeing you."

"Excuse me, sir. But you don't know me at all, so don't let this be about me; its your daughter-in-law who needs you right now."

Gwen came in with the twins just than ran up to Levi eagerly, firing questions about their mother towards him.

"Come on, why don't you two put your things in the truck while I speak to your grandparents?"

The twins agreed quickly and Levi waited until they were out of hearing before he spoke, "Listen, I know you blame Abigail for your son's death, but did you ever think that maybe she tried to stop him from drinking?"

"I don't want to talk about this; you have no right to speak of our son in that way. You never met him; you have no idea who he was!" Gwen said temperamentally pulling Levi towards the door, "Now leave before I call the police."

Levi allowed himself to be pushed out the door and heard the door slam shut behind him as he walked down the marble steps to his truck, the twins sat patiently inside with their bags in the back.

"Are your grandparents always like that?" he asked as they drove down the laneway to the main street.

Cole looked up from where he sat in the passenger seat, "Yes; they don't like us."

"I'm sure they love you both, Cole."

"No, they don't. We aren't allowed to play at their house and they never talk to us," Chloe remarked, twirling a strand of hair around her finger.

How about we go and visit your Mom tomorrow morning? I'm sure she'd love to see you."

The twins readily agreed, anxious to see their mother again. Levi could tell they were nervous about visiting her, especially since she would have no legs. He explained to them as the drove to the apartment about her amnesia, that she might not remember them both because of the accident. They seemed to be very understanding even though.

That night, as Levi tucked Chloe into bed, "Mommy isn't here to say, I love you one hundred M&Ms. I can't sleep without her."

"Oh sweetie, your mother has to get better before she can come home. So you'll have to do with me, jah?" he tweaked her nose, "Do you think you can handle that?"

She giggled, "Yes, I guess so."

"Gut," he exclaimed, "We have to be strong for her, jah?"

"Yes; can we go see her after school?"

Levi nodded, "Jah, your Uncle Mike is going to pick you up from school, okay?"

Chloe accepted that, snuggled down in her bed, and closed her eyes. Levi left her room than and as he switched off the light he watched her turn over in the bed.

Chapter Fourteen

During his physics class the next day, Levi had a very hard time concentrating. Pete had told him that Mr. Hamilton was doing much better and Sean had called to say he had found a lawyer for him. He was to meet Maxwell Smith at the local Coffee Shop that afternoon. So much was on his mind, and he couldn't concentrate on Professor Carter's class. Knowing he would have to speak with him about Larry, he waited after class until he was the only student in the room.

Professor John Carter was a very tall man with only a fringe of white hair covering his balding head. His blue twinkling eyes acknowledged Levi as he walked up.

"Mr. Bontrager, what can I help you with sir?" he asked cheerfully as he put some folding in his briefcase.

Levi shifted from one foot to another, "I'm having trouble with Dr. Larry Fletcher. A patient came in with severe abdominal pain and told me that the pills Larry had given him were not helping. They were Miracure samples and I sent left over pills from the patient to the lab. The results were just a few different vitamins. Later, I overheard Larry and another man arguing about Miracure; and how they want to steal money from the government and patients," He braced his side against the pine desk and folded his arms before him, "Now they have come after my girlfriend and I countless times and have put her in the hospital with serious injuries. The police officer on our case found that the accident she had was not because of her wrong doing but because her brakes were cut."

"Why didn't you come to me sooner?" the professor asked as he at down behind the desk, "We're going to have to place you under someone else and you probably will have to testify in court."

"I know, sir. I have a meeting with Maxwell Smith right now actually."

"That's good. I'm sorry to hear about this Levi," he flipped open a notebook and scribbled something down as he spoke, "How is your friend doing?"

"Not good at all. She lost both of her legs, has two cracked ribs, a concussion, amnesia and a sprained wrist."

Professor Carter stood up and handed him the slip of paper, "Go and see this Doctor. He is always ready to work with new residents. He's a wonderful man; you won't have any problems with him."

"Denki, sir."

"I hope everything works out for you, Levi."

As Levi drove to the Coffee House, he thought about Abby and couldn't wait to see her again later.

Abby groaned and shifted her bound arm to a more comfortable position; she was bored. Aside from the nurses, doctors and her brother's visits, she had nothing to do besides stare up at a white ceiling.

Mike had left a Bible beside her bed, and she had asked the nurse to put it in the drawer by the bed. She had no faith anymore, not since she awoke in the hospital without legs and memory. Life was so complicated now; she had children she couldn't remember and a boyfriend who she only knew because of the memory of his gentle kiss.

The clock on the wall before her read twelve o'clock; lunch time. This meant jello and soup, delicious! Groaning again, she watched as a cafeteria woman with a cap on came in with her lunch tray. The woman smiled at her and made room on her table for the food.

"Good afternoon, Abigail," a bubbly cheerful voice called out. The voice came from a blonde haired nurse in tweety bird scrubs.

She waltzed into the room and lifted the lid off the tray, "This looks very good."

"Huh," Abby muttered grotesquely, "What I would do for some pasta right now."

The nurse laughed and sat on the edge of her bed, "My name is Karen; I'll be your nurse during the days."

Abby said nothing and let her feed her, even though it hurt her pride. With one arm sprained and the other too sore to move because of her cracked ribs, she felt useless. Especially since, she used to be so full of energy.

"So, it must be nice to have such a caring boyfriend, hey? I mean, mine would never do what he has been doing for you and the children," Karen said with a friendly smile, "I don't have any children, but I have seriously been thinking about breaking up with him. But your guy is wonderful."

Swallowing a spoonful of the spicy tomato soup, she mumbled, "Oh sure, he's great. I have no idea who he is, but he's great."

"That must be tough, hey?" she waited until Abby had taken another spoonful before allowing her to respond.

"That hardly touches it. I can deal with having no legs, but no memory? Ugh."

Karen said nothing and after the food was all gone, she checked the bandages and changed them. Once she had left the room, Abby clicked the button for her morphine and drifted off to sleep...

It was raining...and Abby felt scared because had spotted a dark car following her since she had left her apartment. She saw the vehicle draw closer and than ram into her Bronco...

Abby screamed out in fright jerking her body around on the hospital bed. Sweat formed on her brow and tears sprung out of her eyes.

"Abby...Abby, its okay, I'm here," a deep voice spoke gently beside her. Abby opened her eyes to see Levi sitting on the edge of her bed. Crying softly, she turned her face from his view so he wouldn't see her tears.

Levi bent down and gathered her lovingly in his arms, "Ach darlin', its okay."

Abby held herself stiff in his embrace, scared of what she

remembered and scared of him. Somehow, she knew he wasn't the one who hit the car, but she couldn't be sure.

"Did you remember anything?" he asked, leaning back to look in her eyes and wipe the tears from her eyes.

"No," she lied, "Only that I love pasta."

He laughed than, throwing his head back slightly, "Jah, you really do."

A knock sounded on the doorframe and they both turned to see Mike usher the twins into the room. Abby gasped at the sight of the children who held resemblance to Charlie along with their uncle Mike and their Grandma Rose.

"Hello," she called out softly. To her surprise, the twins ran to her and jumped on the bed hugging her tight.

"Mommy, I miss you," Chloe said, sniffling.

Abby blinked as she saw the little girl change to a small baby with laughing eyes and than back to herself. Her memory was coming back after all, it would take time, but it was coming back. If only she could get her legs back.

Levi and Mike went to the cafeteria with Andrea who wasn't ready to see Abby yet. Mike pushed her in her wheelchair and than drew her close to a table.

"What do you want to eat, munchkin?" he asked.

"I just ate, but I'd like some juice." Andrea exclaimed, waving at some friends across the room.

Levi and Mike each ordered a sandwich and a carton of milk with an iced tea for Andrea. The men prayed silently for their food and than set about eating.

"I talked to Maxwell Smith this afternoon, he's pretty sure we have a good chance of winning this case. The paint on Abby's Bronco is a very good start. Sean is looking for Larry right now actually."

Mike listened intently as he spoke and nodded appropriately, while Andrea wheeled herself around to join her group of friends, "I know this must be hard for you, Levi. It'll be hard to live with Abby if you ever plan on marrying."

Levi smiled and held up his hand, palm out, "Hold on, friend. I plan on taking this relationship one step at a time, especially with all that has happened."

He nodded again and than took a bite of his turkey sandwich, chewing slowly. Levi could tell he was battling some inner argument. His face looked drained and his eyes were sunken in.

"You should go home and rest, man. You look exhausted," Levi advised, settling back in his chair.

"Well, you don't look so hot yourself," he snapped, "I advise you to keep your opinions to yourself."

Frowning, Levi said nothing for he knew that he had gone through a lot in the last while. With the passing away of Charlie, than his father and mother and all the incidents around Abby and the children, Mike certainly had much to endure, at both work and home.

The twins were ready to leave when they returned and after they left with Mike for a few hours, Levi sat down next to Abby's bed and took her frail hand in his.

"How are you feeling?"

Abby sighed and pulled her hand from his, "I feel fine; I'm just frustrated and bored."

Levi smiled, "I don't know if I can help with the frustration, but what can I do to help you be less bored?"

She shrugged her shoulders painfully and took in a deep breath, "I don't remember what I like to do, so I don't really care."

"I know you like to read; I could bring you some books from your bookstore."

"Alright."

"If you want, I could read right now. There is a wide selection of books in the patient rec room."

Abby nodded, "Alright."

Chapter Fifteen

Later that night as Levi lay down on the couch reading a book for class, the phone rang in the kitchen bringing him from his studies. Groaning, he jumped up and ran for the phone, stubbing his toe on the corner of the couch as he went by.

"Wow," he muttered as he picked up the receiver, "This is Levi."

"Hello Levi, this is Sean calling. What did you just do?"

Rubbing his toe, Levi took a seat by the table, "Oh, I just stubbed my toe on the couch."

Sean chuckled good naturedly, "Yeah, that'll teach you not to run in the house, eh?"

Levi smiled at his friend's remark, "So, to what do I owe the pleasure of your call?"

He sighed, "We found out that the brakes on Abby's Bronco were definitely cut, but you probably knew that. Also, we have found black paint on the bumper, and one of your forensic scientists found out it is a clear match to Larry's car."

Levi let out a sigh of relief; this was the first real evidence that could help prove the case, "That is big news, Sean. Can you send those results to Maxwell? He'll need them for the case."

"Of course," he replied, "Say hi to Abby and tell her we wish her the best."

"I will Sean."

As he hung up the phone, his cell started to ring in his coat pocket so he went to answer it, "Hello?"

"Levi?"

"Jah. Who is this?"

"Mike; I need a huge favor."

Levi walked back into the kitchen and poured himself a glass of milk as he talked, "Alright, what can I do for you?"

"Can you be with the twins tomorrow? I have to work so I was hoping you could take over for me. I know I said I would baby-sit while you have practicum, but I have no choice. My boss has been ragging me for a while now because I've been taking so much time off."

"That's alright Mike, I'll work something out with Andrea so I can go. She's walking fine now with her crutches." Levi took a bit out of a chocolate chip cookie as he spoke.

After he hung up the phone, Levi went to his room and set about packing up his necessary items. He had practicum tomorrow but the next day was class so he would be home by the time the children got back from school. However, on the days he'd be at the hospital he would need Andrea to stay home and baby-sit.

Later, just as he was almost ready for bed, Levi phoned the hospital to check up on Abby. The nurse assured him that she was sleeping soundly. Although, she had an anger attack when one of the nurses talked to her about the accident and they had to give her something to calm her down. It was a long time before he fell asleep, because of the worry he had about Abby.

The next morning when Levi let himself into Abby's home he was met with chaos. Mike ran after Cole with a comb in his hand and Chloe and Andrea were screaming at each other down the hall. Obviously, Andrea needed more room than usual and Chloe was irritated.

"Hey, what's going on in here?" Levi exclaimed as he set his duffel bag down on the floor.

Immediately Cole stopped in his tracks and Mike grinned quickly at Levi as he held the boy by the shoulders to speak to him.

Mike swiftly combed Cole's unruly hair and than turned to speak to Andrea.

"Where are you going to sleep, Levi?" Cole inquired as he tried to lift the duffel bag from the tiled floor.

"I think I will be sleeping in your mother's room, Cole. Is that alright with you, son?"

He nodded, puffing out his little chest, "Sure, it sure would nice to have another man around here."

Levi hid a smile beneath his hand at the forwardness of the child. After putting his duffel bag aside, he called the twins and Andrea into the kitchen and than put on a pot of coffee for Mike and himself.

"So, Andrea, I have a proposition for you," he announced over his shoulder as he flicked the on button of the coffee maker.

Andrea, who was reading the funnies in the newspaper, put it down and looked up at him with her mysterious eyes, "Oh, yeah?"

"I would like you to baby-sit the twins on Mondays, Wednesdays, and Fridays, when I have practicum. I'll compensate you for it by buying you art supplies." Levi sat down across from her and stretched his legs under the table, "So, it's a good deal, jah?"

She shrugged, "It's not like I have anything better to do right now."

Levi took a key from off his key chain, "I made a copy of the key to the house so you can go out for groceries and meet the bus. Make sure the twins do their homework everyday before they play jah?"

She nodded and took the keys from him, "Can I ask you something, Levi?"

"Jah, what is it?"

"How is Mom going to come home in her wheelchair? The stairs are winding and narrow and there is hardly any space up here."

Mike sat down beside Andrea than and handed Levi a mug of coffee, "We're renovating Grandma's house so it'll be big enough and more open. Right now we've put all the furniture in a storage room so we can work."

"Really? Will my room be bigger?" Chloe asked eagerly as she took a sip from her orange juice."

Levi smiled and ruffled the little girl's hair, "We'll see what we can do, alright?"

That seemed to curb her curiosity and than Andrea exclaimed loudly, "Time for the bus, let's go."

The twins gave them all a quick hug and than ran outside to meet the bus on time. Andrea went to her room to paint and Mike and Levi cleaned up the dishes. Once Mike left, Levi took his bags to Abby's room.

As he unpacked his things, Levi looked around Abby's room and tears came to his eyes. Little knick knacks were scattered here and there all over the room. A pink sweater he remembered her wearing the first time he saw her in the store, lay over a chair in the corner. Levi sat on the edge of the bed and opened the top drawer of her night table. A worn Bible, a diary and an album full of pictures occupied the small space, so he opened the Bible to where the marker sat and started to read.

It was later that day when he realized he had not returned the cigar box to his Dat. It was something that he had been prolonging because he knew that an argument would eventually surface when they spoke. However, it seemed like the least he could do for Abby's mother. Andrea was happy to baby-sit the twins for the evening, so after dinner he took a quick shower and than headed over to his parents' home.

As he drove through the familiar neighborhood, he recognized special places from his childhood. There was an old swamp where he used to fish with Abe, a forest where they made a fort, and of course, the little backwoods cabin. The closer he became to his childhood home, the more edgy he became. What would his Dat say when he came in the house? Would he be angry? Or, would they be civil this time? Taking in a deep breath, Levi turned his truck down the rutted laneway leading to the white washed farm home.

No sooner had he parked his truck along side the home, than an elderly man with a long white beard and black hat poked his head out from inside the barn. Since Levi had not seen his Dat in many years, it was a shock to see how old he had become. Slowly, he ventured out of the safety of his truck and made his way over to his Dat, who now had brought himself into Levi's vision.

"Levi, is that you?" he asked with a perplexed look on his rugged face.

Levi stopped a few feet away from him, "Jah Dat, it's me."

His Dat looked down at his feet and than back toward his son, "It has been many years, Levi. What brings you back to our home?"

Noticing that he did not refer the home as Levi's, he explained softly, "I have somethin' that needed to be returned to you. The mother of my girlfriend Abby used to be a gut friend of yours and she asked me to give you your cigar box back."

"A friend of mine, you say?" Mr. Bontrager frowned and gestured for Levi to come inside the house, "Well, let us go and see if your Ma has something for us men to drink, jah?"

Levi couldn't believe what he was hearing; was he finally being asked to join the family again? As he followed his Dat's feeble steps up to the house, he suddenly felt like a heavy weight was being lifted from his shoulders.

Catherine Bontrager stood at the kitchen counter cutting up a lemon sponge cake, and Levi recalled how many times he had watched her from the table. Only now she was hunched over with graying hair and wrinkles, but what a beautiful picture she still made.

"Ma, Levi is home." Dat grunted, taking off his hat and hanging it on a peg by the door, "Can you pour us some coffee, we men have some talkin' to do."

Before Levi could even venture into the room, his mother rounded the table and enveloped him in her loving arms, "Oh Levi child, it is wonderful-gut to see you again. It has been too long."

Tears sprang forth from his eyes as he clung to his mother, "Jah, it is very gut to be back."

"What is this about you needin' to talk with your Dat and not me?" she asked sharply, stepping back from his embrace.

Levi smiled at his mother's forwardness, "I have met a wonderful-gut woman, Ma. She has twins and a stepdaughter whom I have come to love. Her mother was a very close friend of Dat's and she asked me to return something of his."

"Are you talking about Rose?" she asked, glancing from him to his Dat.

Mr. Bontrager blushed and sat down at the table, "I would assume so, Ma."

Levi sat beside his father and handed him the box and a bag with pictures. He watched as his father's eyes filled with tears and than looked at his mother who was placing a cup of coffee before them.

"She was quite a woman, that Rose." Abram looked toward his son as he spoke, "I am sorry that I did not tell you about my rompspringe with her. Jah, we were very much in love and I planned to marry her. But your Ma, who had been working on our farm kept distracting me from Rose. It wasn't long before Rose caught on and left and I gave in to Ma's quest."

"Is that so, Abram? You say I was the one who followed you around?" Levi had to chuckle at his Ma who stood with her hands on her ample hips, "I recall one spring morning' where you stayed at my side for an entire day while I planted seeds in the garden. You even helped me, and when this Rose girl came over, you made up an excuse that you had to work."

Again, his Dat blushed crimson and Levi and his mother laughed mercilessly. From than on, they sat together at the table recalling stories from the past and it wasn't long before Levi had spilled the entire ordeal about Abby's accident. They felt so bad for what had happened, that they decided to go and visit her in the hospital. It seemed to Levi that the shame of the shunning was not interrupting their bonds.

Levi finally drove back to the apartment at eleven o'clock with two pies and his Ma's special Waldorf salad. When he got back, he immediately filled himself a bowl and ate the delicious concoction as bedtime snack. It was a great ending to the day.

The new doctor Levi was assigned to work in a free clinic in the east end where many underprivileged families lived. Doctor Dean McBride, an elderly stooped over man, met him at the door when he arrived for his first day.

"Hello, you must be Resident Levi Bontrager," he announced with a friendly smile, "I'm glad to have an extra pair of hands around here."

Levi shook his hand enthusiastically, "And I am glad those hands belong to me, sir."

Doc McBride, as he was asked to call him, immediately pulled him along for a tour of the facility, "The front room here is the waiting area, we have a section for the children to play as well," he gestured to the large expanse already full of parents and crying children, elderly folk and pregnant woman. "Since we are the only free clinic around these parts, we are pretty much always crammed full, so don't expect any free time for assignments while you're here."

Although Doc McBride was getting on in his years he was surprisingly efficient in his work and compassionate to the patients needs. Many of the patients were financially in trouble and were unable to get any other care, so they came to the free clinic.

By the end of his shift, Levi felt like his legs were lead and he could barely keep his eyes open. Even though Doc McBride had told him he would only be observing on this first shift; he had started one his own by lunch. Levi went into the staff room to collect his briefcase and dishes. He checked his cell phone and noted that Pete had called, so he sat down his things on the table and called his friend from the office phone.

A laugh sounded on the phone as someone picked up, "Hello."

"Is this Pete?"

"Yes, who may I ask is calling?"

Levi smiled to himself, "Oh, now I'm disappointed, you can't even recognize my…"

"Levi, hey, you called back," he interrupted excitedly.

"Jah, so are you going to tell me what you wanted?"

Pete laughed, "I just wanted to tell you that Larry made a huge commotion at the hospital because you weren't there to work."

Levi smirked and tapped his fingers on the table top, "Really, I wonder why he still would want me to work for him."

"Keep your friends close and your enemies closer, Levi."

"Right; denki for letting me know, Pete."

"It's no problem. Take care, buddy."

Levi said goodbye and than collected his things and went out to his truck. However, when he stepped around the corner of the building and onto the sidewalk, nothing could have prepared him for the sight before him. Directly in front of him, spray painted on the length of his truck, were the words in red, 'Back off!'

Anger flashed inside as he kicked the front tire of the truck, he could not tolerate any more of the disaster headed in his direction each day. Inside he had always felt that forgiveness was the best path to go on, but in this situation, he could not agree with his earlier argument. Levi jumped into his truck and called Sean on his cell phone.

After Sean answered with a brisk hello, Levi told him that he could not handle any more of the craziness and that he wanted to meet at the ballpark to discuss a proper course of action. His friend exclaimed that he would get the men together and meet him there.

Chapter Sixteen

Levi parked his truck near the bleachers and watched as a group of men came walking towards him. Mike, Todd, Sean, Patrick and James Fordwick (brothers who worked for Sean) and some of Todd's crew.

"Denki for coming. I know that you all probably had other things to attend to before coming here, but the fact of the matter is, I can't go on like this much longer," Levi pointed to the angry words displayed over his truck, "We need to do something before this gets even more out of hand."

Sean pushed a hand through his hair and nodded, "I agree Levi, we've haven't been doing enough. While driving out here I though about what we could do, and I think I might have an idea."

The men pressed closer to hear the plan, "Now Levi, you told me that Allan was his accomplice right?"

"That's right."

"Well, we haven't come up with anything out of the order with Larry yet because he's smart about hiding things. However, Allan is less sneaky and he might make a mistake that we can catch. All we need to do is place some men in front of his place to watch and we can bring him in for something."

Levi crossed his arms before him and leaned back against the truck, "What have you found out about him so far?"

Patrick tucked his hands into the pockets of his jeans, "Well, he grew up in this area and went to our schools and than when he graduated he went to Boston where he lived with relatives while he studied for his medical degree. He met Trisha Coldwell their and a year later they were married; they moved here as soon as he finished school. He's had a clean record, not even a speeding ticket."

"I guess it wouldn't hurt to have some men staked out in front of his house."

Sean nudged Patrick as he responded, "If nothing happens we can do a little something to stir things up; nothing illegal but something to drag him out into the open."

They all chuckled and than Levi pointed into the truck, where he had put the pizzas he had picked up and they all dug in.

Levi went to Abby's apartment and found Andrea sitting on the couch with a book on her lap. The only light in the room came from the lamp on the table beside her, and the glow illuminated on her face.

"How are the children?" he asked as he shrugged out of his coat and hung it on the hook by the door.

Andrea put her book aside and stood up, "They've been asleep since seven; Uncle Mike took them to see Mom."

Nodding, Levi emptied his lunch containers onto the kitchen counter; "How is your foot doing?"

"It feels stiff but otherwise not so bad."

"Well, I'm heading off to bed, Andrea, I've got to get up early because I want to see your mother before I go to work."

Early the next morning on Rosewood Drive, east of the Churchville Elementary School the two brothers in the police force waited anxiously in a dark sedan for any sign of life at the Welling home. Patrick looked at his brother who sat sleeping with his head against the window, "Hey lazy bones, we don't get paid to sleep, you know," he remarked, giving James a shove.

James stretched his arms out and than rubbed his eyes, "What time is it?"

The two brothers were alike in looks, with their blonde hair, blue eyes, and tall frame. However, when it came to character, they were definitely from a different pod. Patrick tended to be commanding and pushy; he loved being the leader of a group and continued to prove his point. Whereas James was a hot-tempered man of adventure; and he had a very comical behavior. Everyone liked him, even though he loved to talk up a debate. Yet when it came to the law, both men were alike in their belief in it.

"It's about time for Allan to head for work and the children will be going to school in a half hour."

"I'm hungry; do you think we could get something to eat later?" James asked, rubbing his growling stomach.

Patrick grimaced and shook his head, "Do you always have to think with your stomach?"

"No, but I need a full stomach to think. I sure hope the next shift gets here soon, I've got a hankering for some of Maud's pancakes."

"You always have a hankering for her pancakes, James, but The Churchville Café will be open all day and she'll make you pancakes at any time so don't fret."

James was just about to respond when the front door to the Robertson household opened and a young woman with blonde hair walked onto the veranda. The garage door opened next and Allan's blue Jeep Cherokee pulled out and stopped as the door went shut.

"Looks like the next shift has arrived, we'll have to pull out." Patrick said, starting the car up, "We'll just follow this guy and see where he goes, maybe he'll meet Larry somewhere."

The CB radio went on and the other team told them to head out. Patrick pulled the car up around the corner and waited for Allan to come; a few seconds later, they followed him out towards the interstate.

Levi had a good visit with Abby; they had talked together about the future and what it entailed for her as well his himself. He knew that it would never be the same as he had first thought, but it didn't matter as long as she was alive and well. Since she had been getting tired of hospital food, Levi had brought some bagels and cream cheese. They had a nice breakfast and than it was time for him to go to work.

Now as he drove toward the clinic he thought about how lonely it must be for her in the hospital. For a person like Abby, the best way to heal would be if she were around her family. Somehow, he was going to have to see about homecare after the house was remodeled. As he turned the corner onto Main Street, Levi's cell phone rang out and he had to park along side the road to answer it.

"Gut daag," he said in his former speech.

"Hello Levi, this is Sean. I just wanted to let you know that Patrick and James followed Mort to a café outside Churchville. He was there meeting Larry and they seemed to be talking very seriously and even got into an argument. The boys have it all on tape and they're bringing them in, so I thought I'd let you know about it."

Levi smiled in thanksgiving, "Oh that is good news Sean. Thank you for calling. Let me know when you get finished with the interrogation, jah?"

"Why don't you come and listen in? They won't be able to tell that you are there anyways, you'll be behind the glass wall."

"I don't know, Sean. My work is pretty important right now, I have to work to get my points, and I need points to graduate."

"Oh you can come in after work; we can let them rot it out in a cell for a few hours. They might be a little freer to speak later on this way."

They both laughed and Levi told him he would be by directly after work. Before he pulled back on the street, Levi felt a burden slide off his shoulders and he prayed reverently to God, thanking Him for His Grace.

The room facing the interrogation room was cold and dark. Levi stood with his shoulder against the wall, watching Larry sit anxiously in a chair by the long table. He seemed nervous, his hands constantly moving in front of him and his beady eyes darting back and forth. Sean walked into the room than with a lawyer who sat next to Larry, obviously working for him.

"You warm enough, Dr. Fletcher? What about water; are you thirsty?" Sean asked as he slapped a file of papers down on the tabletop.

Larry growled, "There's no need for you to be civil Chief, I know how you feel about me. Leaving me in that cell for hours; do you do that to all your criminals?"

Sean smirked, "Are you saying you're a criminal than? I guess our work here is finished, you've already admitted to a crime that hasn't been brought forward."

"You know what he means, officer," The anxious lawyer exclaimed, "Just get to the point."

"What I would like to know is about this new medication you are promoting. A lot of evidence points to you in certain criminal actions and we have finally made a good discovery as to your intentions with this medication." Sean stood up and walked around the table to sit in front of him, "Frankly, I am amazed at your ideas. Although they may seem smart to you, it is very dense. You see, once we have you in for suspicion of the selling of drugs, the men who are expecting huge shipments of these capsules will be angry because of the money you owe them. They will come after you and ruin your family, your practice, and every thread of the life you have achieved for yourself."

Levi gasped from his side of the glass; he had not thought that Larry could be involved in the drug cartel. However, it all made perfect sense. By promoting this medication, he could serve two worlds and make double or triple the money. It was no wonder that he came after them and tried to get them to be quiet.

"You're not going to get anything out of me that you don't have." Larry exclaimed, "So you might as well forget about doing the bad cop, good cop routine."

"We'll just have to see what your friend Mort has to say. We've got him in the next room, and I'm sure you know how his mouth tends to run off when he gets nervous."

Larry scoffed and shrugged, "He won't say anything because the life of his family depends on it. He knows that the minute he speaks up they'll be dead."

Sean stood up and walked around the table, "Well, we'll just see what your dear little friend has to say and than we'll talk, alright?"

From behind the glass window, Levi watched as Sean picked up the file on the table and walked from the room. Larry slammed his fist on the table and grunted in frustration. Clearly, Sean had hit a nerve before walking from the room; otherwise, he would not have shown emotion that clear.

Levi followed to the next interrogation room and remained behind the glass wall just as before. The man seated behind the table looked anxious. Sweat poured down his balding head, his beady eyes convulsing, and his chunky hands jittering before him. Sean entered the room and handed Allan a bottle of water before sitting in front of him.

"Okay Allan, why don't you tell me exactly what you've been up too. If you tell us everything we will be much easier on you, and you might just have a chance at a lighter sentence. What do you say, huh?"

Allan leaned his head on his cuffed hands, "If I talk, my family will die. How can I be sure that you will protect them?"

"You are just going to have to trust us, Allan." Sean took the cap off the water bottle and handed to him, "Take a drink, you look dehydrated."

"Fine, I'll speak, but only when I know my family is safe."

Sean came out of the interrogation room a few minutes later and Levi followed him to the desk quarters. One of the secretaries brought some dinner in and everyone dug into the Chinese food. Levi's was amazed when Sean prayed for everyone before eating and read a portion of the Bible afterwards. Than, later when all the food cartons were cleared away and files were splayed over the table, he explained the situation to everyone.

"The only safe house in town is pretty well full now, so we can't get the information we need right away. Unless, of course, one you feel up to the responsibility of caring and protecting this family," Sean stood in the front of the room looking down at his colleagues, "We need to get this perp to talk; he's our only chance."

Levi took a sip of the coffee in the mug before him, "Why don't they stay in my old apartment? I'm not staying there right now."

"Alright, we'll park a squad car in front to keep watch and they should be safe. In the mean time, we should get Allan's testimony starting at the beginning."

An hour later, Levi was once again seated behind the glass wall watching Sean talking to Allan and his lawyer. Allan had agreed to the plan and was about to give the names of the drug lords who had already paid for the capsules. Over twenty individuals had signed up with them and they were well-known drug distributors. Sean was excited about the information he was getting because they had been trying to track these men down for a very long time.

Levi was excited when he received a call from Doc McBride saying that they would be working in the ER for the next few months. The nurses union had gone on strike and the clinic had to close during the duration of the issue. The ER had always been a place where Levi wanted to work as a Pediatrician and he was glad that he would finally get the chance to observe Doc McBride in surgery. As a young man, Doc McBride had been in Pediatrics, but as he got older he decided to cover the medicinal charts rather than surgical. However, since the shortage of nurses had occurred, he decided he had little chance.

The ER was a very demanding place but Levi immediately felt at home. As an intern, he had a lot to learn, but he was excited to be able to observe the masters at work. Dr. David Henderson and Dr. Susan O'Leary were the two Residents that had always captured his attention and he was happy to be working along side them.

"Bontrager, would you care to assist me in Trauma three?" Doc McBride questioned, "We have a five year old girl with AIDS."

Levi followed his mentor into the small room where a small girl lay on a stretcher. She looked small for the age of five. Her mother sat next to her holding her frail hand. Immediately Doc McBride introduced himself and than Levi and asked about the symptoms.

"Jayne has been throwing up and she has a bad fever. I can't get her to eat anything either. What is wrong, Doc?" the mother explained nervously, "I'm just getting so nerved up about this all."

He turned his graying head toward Levi, "What do you think, Bontrager? What is the procedure that needs to be made?"

Holding the chart in front of him, Levi flipped through the pages as he spoke, "I believe a lumbar puncture would be in Jayne's best interest, it would help find the right kind of medication to be administered."

"Good," was the Doc's response, "Now, explain to Mrs. Robson what this means. I'm sure she would like to be informed about the procedure."

"Well, we will put two needles into the spine; the first is the numb the area and the second is to take a sample."

Doc McBride nodded, "Right, we will start immediately Mrs. Robson. You can stay here and talk to her while we work; we need her to stay calm."

A nurse came in to assist setting up the surgical area, and than Levi cleaned the area before inserting the first needle. Jayne whimpered and moved around as he worked, but between her mother's calm words and Doc McBride's assurance, she settled down by the time the second needle needed to be inserted.

By the instructions of his mentor, Levi waited by the bedside until the Lab results came back. Levi talked to Jayne for a while about school, her friends and AIDS. When the nurse came in with the results, Levi groaned as he read them and than went to find Doc McBride.

"They did a cell count, differential, protein, glucose, Gram's stain and culture, but they ran out of fluid before the India ink." Levi explained a few minutes later as they walked back to Trauma 3.

Doc McBride groaned, "That means we'll need to do another lumbar. Let's talk to the mother and explain the necessity."

It took another half hour to get the extra sample and than the two men went to do the India ink.

"Okay, so what do you do first, Levi?"

"Put three drops of the fluid on the scope and than the ink. Than we slide it under the microscope."

"Right, and what do you see?" Doc McBride leaned over as he spoke and watched as Levi looked through the scope.

"Yeast cells, and some capsules around them."

"Cryptococcus."

"She has cryptococcal Meningitis?"

Doc McBride nodded and massaged his forehead, "Yeah."

Levi shook his head sadly, "That means she's near the end."

They returned to Jayne's room and told the bad news and than explained that they would have to do a reverse spinal tap twice a day for ten days to fight the infection. The mother cried in grief and Levi had to take her from the room and comfort her.

As they sat in the private waiting area talking, she asked Levi if he could read a portion from the Bible and pray with her. Levi took a Bible off a shelf filled with medical books and than sat beside her, opening it to Psalm 30.

"I will extol thee, O Lord; for thou hast lifted me up, and hast not made my foes to rejoice over me. O Lord my God, I cried unto thee, and thou hast healed me. O Lord thou hast brought up my soul from the grave: thou hast kept me alive, that I should not go down to the pit…"

Levi continued to read the small passage and his eyes filled up with tears. Although he had meant to help the mother with her inward pain, he also found the words to calm his heart and thoughts as well. He had not received as much time to spend with Abby as he wished he could; he made a pact with himself that he would go see her after work and tell her about the investigation. In his heart he missed her more than he could find the words to say; she was everything to him and he needed her like bees need nectar.

"Thank you, Doctor, for doing this for me. You are not a regular physician, you are human being." Jayne's mother broke him from his thoughts and patted his hand in thanks, "I feel comforted by your words and the passage you picked. It fit the moment perfectly, thank you."

Levi smiled, "There is no need to thank me, ma'am; those words were comforting to me also. I hope everything turns out okay for you and your beautiful daughter. Let me know if I can help, jah?"

She smiled than, amidst tears of joy, "I'll call you without a doubt, sir. I'm sure we will have questions now and again."

They walked together back to Jayne's room and found her reading, 'Green Eggs and Ham,' by Doctor Zeus. Levi checked her vitals, gave instructions to the nurse and than went to check with Doc McBride.

Abby sat in a wobbly wheelchair by the window, watching children playing outside in the yard behind the rehab center. She was glad Mike had made the plans for her transfer to this facility. It was not near as busy and crowded as the hospital; and they hosted the best physicians and therapists. In addition, they had a great yard where the family could visit; there was a huge pool for muscle strengthening and a tennis court, baseball field and basketball court. Clients from the facility were scattered all over the yard, and Abby watched them struggle to move around. She drew in a deep breath and let it out in a shaky puff. Would she ever be able to walk again?

Chapter Seventeen

A soft knock on the door broke her from the anxious thoughts and she turned to see Levi leaning up against the doorframe. His large form seeming to take up more space than reality; she had almost forgotten how handsome he was. He looked at her intently as a soft smile crept across his tanned face; he was beautiful.

"Hey," he said softly as he pushed off the doorframe and sauntered across the room towards her. He took a seat on the bed next to her chair and turned it towards him as he leaned in for a kiss.

She murmured a light, "Hello," against his lips and than kissed him back lightly, "I missed you, Levi."

He leaned back slightly, his brows arched, "You did?

"Yeah, I am so sorry about the way I have been acting lately." She twirled a finger in the dark curls around his ears, "I love you so much, and I should have been strong and fought."

Levi shook his head and placed a hand on either side of her face, "No, you were already strong for me, Abby. It was wrong of me to drag you into all of this anyway and I'm sorry for what happened. This was all my fault; I should have just left it to the police."

Abby giggled and kissed him quickly, "Oh, you know you are too stubborn for that, don't you?"

They chuckled together and than Levi asked her if she wanted to go outside and he pushed her in the chair out to the lawn. He carried her to a blanket on the floor and carefully set her down so as not to irritate her bandages. Everything that had happened in the last while seemed to float away and they drank wine, ate a good meal that Levi had picked up and than Levi read to her from Tennyson poems. By the time they were ready to go inside, it was turning dark. Levi promised to be back the next day with the children and kissed her good night by her door as the nurse came in to give her medication.

That night, Abby read from a book that Mike had brought over from her store. The story was a remarkable love story and she was soon drawn completely into the theme. As she read, she thought of no one else except the characters in the book. She didn't even notice the nurse come in and check her vitals and bandages as she lay on the bed. However, she was soon interrupted by a loud hello and she had to tear herself away from the book.

A tall blonde haired man stood beside her bed with a bright smile on her face, "Did I interrupt you from a good book?"

Nodding, she watched as he pulled a chair close to her bed, "Yes, you did. Who are you?"

"My name is Spencer Miller and I am going to be your physical therapist. Your doctor has informed me that you will soon be able to start strengthening your muscles and we want to get you moving again." He opened a file he had on his lap, "Abigail, you have to tell me if you will lend yourself wholly to me and do what ever I tell you when we begin. Can you do that?"

Abby shrugged, "I guess so; when do we begin?"

A small smile crept across his handsome face, "We'll start in two days, alright? Tomorrow you have an appointment with a counselor who will be telling you what to expect in the future. You'll be seeing her every day while you're in here and she'll just talk to you and help you prepare a few goals to reach."

"What's she like?"

"Peyton is an amazing woman, I'm sure you will get along with her just fine. You have no cause to be nervous."

Spencer handed her some papers to sign and than he left with the promise of coming two days later. Abby looked over the papers he had left with her and groaned at the extent of the therapy she would be having. It was not going to be a piece of cake that was for sure.

Chapter Eighteen

The following morning, Abby ate her breakfast with gusto and than talked to the nurse as she checked her bandages and gave the medication. Her name was Kelly and she had just finished her nursing degree, which had been a challenge with a husband and three children at home. After she left the room, Abby opened her book to where she had left off and was about to start reading when a woman whirled into her room. Her red hair was tied up in the back and locks of escaped hair framed her face.

"Hello Abigail, my name is Peyton Kingston and I am going to be your councilor. Would you like to sit in a wheelchair while we talk? It will be good to get you out of that bed." She gestured toward the two nurses who had followed her into the room and they helped her into the chair while Payton continued to talk.

"So, I heard that you met Spencer last night and he told you about my coming her to see you." She took a seat directly in front of Abby and opened up a binder filled with information, "What we are going to do today is probably the most painful session we will be having together, but I find that once we get this out of the way we can concentrate on other things."

Abby rubbed her forehead as she felt a headache coming, "Okay, let's just get this over with than."

Peyton took her hands in her own, "I know you probably don't really like this; none of my patients do at first. But, once we get through the first session you will find it very relieving."

For the next hour, she explained to Abby what to expect in the next few months. First, she would go through grueling physical therapy and once the wound had healed neatly, they would start practicing on her prosthetic leg. Things would than start to flow from there. She would be frustrated, angry with herself and others and she would have a hard time around her family. Abby grew very anxious at the thought of this and felt that she would not be able to accomplish what needed to be done in order to get her life back on track.

"I know that this all seems like a tough mountain to climb; but we just have to find the right path. And if an obstacle gets in our way we will just have to use our mind to choose the method easiest to take."

For the next few minutes, they wrote up some goals for her to obtain and than Peyton pushed her outside in the wheelchair so she could enjoy the fresh air before lunch.

Levi was just getting out the shower when his pager started to beep; it was Sean. He flipped on a pair of jeans and a black t-shirt before running out of the bathroom to use the phone in the kitchen. Andrea sat at the table with the twins who were doing their homework.

"I'm going to be on an important phone call, so you need to be quiet," he exclaimed as he picked up the receiver and dialed the familiar numbers.

As he waited for Sean to answer, he listened to Cole talk about their visit with Abby the day before. They had gone for a walk outside and the children were able to swim in the pool while Abby read at the waterside. He could tell that they were relaxed and confident now, which happened to be a big step from the resilient days past.

"Levi?" Sean questioned suddenly, bringing his attention back to the phone call. This was obviously something very serious, because his pager was only used or emergencies.

"Jah, I got your page. What happened?" Levi took a sip of the glass of orange juice Andrea had set before him on the counter.

He sighed, "It's bad. I had some men track Allan when he was released yesterday and he had some visitors late last night. We believe that they belong to the cartel and are asking questions. The family hasn't left the house and neither have the men. I think that we are having a hostage situation going on."

Levi slammed his fist on the counter and than winced in pain, "Aww man, what next? What do you plan to do?"

"I've got a friend who is a hostage negotiator and he's heading over to the house now. I just wanted to give you a heads up and advise you to lock your doors and not leave the house. If some of the men are getting antsy, it is a sure sign that there will be more of them heading in your direction once they get the lowdown of the situation. I'll send over a group patrol, so you should be safe."

"Alright," Levi's heart started to race and he suddenly thought about Abby, "Can you send some men over to Abby also?"

"I won't let anyone touch her, Levi. You have my word. I have to go now and brief my men, but I'll keep you updated on the situation."

Levi hung up the phone after a quick goodbye and than herded the children into the living room, "I want you all to stay in here while I go lock up the store and house. I just got a call and we have to keep watch for anything out of the ordinary."

Cole rubbed his nose with his fingertips and looked up at Levi as he sat on the couch, "What is out of the ordinary?"

"Anything that doesn't seem like it normally does." Levi went down on his haunches in front of the twins, while Andrea took a seat in the recliner. "Everyday you go to school and come home at the same time? What always stays the same every day other than that?"

"When we close the store… or eat dinner…or do our homework?" Chloe exclaimed with a questioning gaze.

Levi pulled on one of her pigtails, "That's right, sweetie. So, when you see something out of the ordinary, you will let me know, right?"

The twins nodded and than shifted backwards on the couch to get comfortable. Andrea looked at him anxiously and than got up and sat beside the twins, "Do what you have to do, I'll stay with them."

Downstairs, as Levi drew the shades at the front of the store, he watched the street carefully to look for any suspicious activity. Outside, the Pennsylvania skies were turning to a dark grey as wild clouds rolled in. Levi watched as a soft rain began to fall and realized that it felt just like the weather was in tune with his feelings. It was scary to think that dangerous men could be coming after him. His life had been so simple, so plain before his marriage. Of course, he knew he had made the right choice in leaving the community; but was it so wrong to wish he were back amidst the safe enclosure.

Levi was just closing the blinds in the front window, when he saw something out of the corner of his eye. Two men stood across the street in long trench coats, smoking, and looking in his direction. He closed the blinds and than moved two blinds apart to take a closer look. One of the men was big and very tall, his face was shadowed over by the other man, who was thin and wrangely. He seemed somewhat nervous and agitated.

It didn't take long for Levi to call Sean and give him the news. Sean advised him to call Mike and see if he could put a name to the faces.

Mike, who was working on his computer, asked Levi to go on to Abby's laptop and than wait for Mike to hack in. It wasn't long before Levi could see Mike's face on a web camera and than they were able to talk freely.

"Is everything alright over there?" Mike asked, waving his hand in their direction. His face was haggard, like he had not had much sleep and the lines under his eyes were tremendously noticeable.

Levi nodded, "We're okay for now. Andrea's reading to the twins in the living room, but there are some people hanging out across the street and it just doesn't add up. Could you check them out?"

Mike connected to the FBI criminal base and some names flew across the screen, "Here is a list of all the men in the drug cartel; they happen to be hiding very well and seem to have a lot of experience flying under the radar. These men used to smuggle drugs across the border by implanting them in human bodies, but we've caught so many that they are looking for other ways to do business. We just haven't been able to connect them to the crimes yet. Why don't you take a picture of these men and send it my way. I can do a facial recognition and tell you if it matches any of the men in the cartel."

"Jah, that sounds like a wonderful gut idea. Hang tight; I'll be back in a bit."

Andrea was able to locate a digital camera for him and she handed it over with a questioning gaze. But Levi did not want to get her scared, so he just told her to go back to the children. She scowled at him, but shuffled out of the kitchen anyway.

Back at the front window downstairs, Levi snapped a few pictures of the men who still stood in the same area as before. He than ran back upstairs and sent Mike the pictures over the computer.

"The pictures are not very good, but I hope it will work out okay."

Mike chuckled, "Well Levi, you don't know me so well yet, but you shouldn't underestimate my powers mister."

They both laughed and Levi watched as he digitally enhanced the photos, "Wow, you really are great at this."

It only took a few minutes before they had two names to connect them to the faces, Antonio Fabrio and Carlo Sanchez. They were wanted for drug trafficking, possession of firearms and smuggling. "They sure have a long rap sheet, Levi. I'm sending this over to Sean right now. He'll know what to do."

A few minutes after Sean disconnected, the phone rang and it was Sean. They were sending an undercover patrol car to follow them if or when they gave up.

After hanging up the phone, Levi called the kids into the kitchen and asked if they wanted a smoothie. They had put up with his tough attitude all evening, so he decided they deserved a treat.

"Is everything alright, Levi?" Andrea asked with another questioning brow. She was cutting strawberries in quarters as he poured milk into the blender.

"Jah, I think so. At least, I hope so. However, until I get the okay from Sean, you have to be very cautious. Especially when you go to school; if you see anything, and I mean anything, out of the ordinary, you call."

Cole grinned as he popped a piece of strawberry into his mouth, "Mommy bought us cell phones a while ago. She said they were only in case of emergency. But I think we have to buy time or something."

Andrea rolled her eyes, "Buy minutes, you mean."

"That's what I said, silly."

Levi pulled out a fifty-dollar bill and handed to Andrea, "I want you to go to the store in the morning and buy some those minutes, okay. Are these phones on Telus?"

"I think so, Mom has them in a drawer in her room," she replied, "I seen them when I was packing her clothes for the hospital."

Sure enough, he found them safely tucked in the back of her sock drawer; still the Telus packaging. It took a while to program the emergency numbers in the phones, and when he returned to the kitchen, he found them at the table. Each child held a glass between their hands and sipped the strawberry smoothie through a straw.

Levi took a seat next to Cole and took a large sip of the ice cold drink. His head immediately froze and he yelped in surprise. The twins started to giggle, but Andrea just rolled her eyes and looked into her glass as she drank.

Later, when the twins were sound asleep on the couch and Andrea was reading in her room, he decided to give Abby a call.

At the sound of her soft voice, his heart jumped and he had to catch his breath. He had never experienced such a jolt in any other relationship he had, "Levi, I'm so glad you called."

"How is everything going over there, Abby? Have you noticed anything peculiar happening?" he asked immediately.

It took a few seconds for her to respond, "What's going on Levi? Sean called and he sent two men to watch over me. They hardly let me go to the washroom, and when I need to go its serious business. Without legs it's a tough job; it takes over a half hour just to go there."

Levi heard sadness in her voice and than asked calmly, "Is everything alright, honey? You sound sad."

"I am sad, Levi." She retorted in an angry rush, "I can't understand how you still love me; I'm an invalid and if we marry I would bring so many problems to our marriage."

He sighed and settled back in the recliner, "Abby, honey, I know we will have problems, but every marriage has them. I love you and that will not change. You're mothers house is being remodeled and it looks wonderful. The entire bottom floor is wheelchair equipped and the counters are nice and low so you can wheel around easy. There is lots of room now."

Abby started to sob, "I just don't understand you, Levi. You are so wonderful, what did I ever do to deserve you?"

They chatted for a few minutes longer but than Sean's number showed up on the call display, so Levi said a quick goodbye and answered his call.

"Sean, what's up?"

"We've got Patrick and his brother tailing Antonio and Carlo, and they're heading to the old warehouses where we went before. I'll keep you updated on our progress, but right now, you can relax."

"Denki, Sean. At least I might be able to catch a few decent winks tonight."

Levi carried the twins, one at a time, to their room and laid them on their beds. Than he said good night to Andrea and headed off to bed.

Chapter Nineteen

Two days later, Levi awoke to the aroma of pancakes and sausage drifting from the kitchen. At first, he thought he was dreaming, and turned over to go back to sleep, but when the aroma continued to hang in the area, he opted to investigate.

Cole and Chloe were standing on a chair at the counter, watching and singing while Andrea poured batter into a frying pan. They all looked in his direction and he had to smile. They looked so adorable covered in flour and batter. The day before had been very strenuous on them. He had brought them to school and come to work late, just to be sure that they were safe. Than he left work early to pick them up, but Mike had already come and left with them. Sean had phoned and told him that the patrol was still at the warehouse to keep an eye on Antonio and Carlos. When the children had gotten home later that night, Levi played Scrabble with them and Andrea went to her room to talk to her friend on the phone. They had a very busy day, so he had said nothing when she was still chatting an hour later. Cole and Chloe did their homework and crawled into bed without a word of refusal, and Levi was happy to follow in their steps.

"Gut morning all." He greeted, taking a seat at the table, "Why are you all up so early?"

Andrea smiled over her shoulder at him, "We heard that it is your birthday today, so we thought we'd make you breakfast."

Levi gasped, covering his mouth with his hand in surprise, "My birthday? I completely forgot about it."

Chloe giggled, "How can you forget your birthday?"

"I don't know pumpkin; maybe I was just too caught up in everything that's been going on." Levi stood up and set out four placemats and than started to disperse the dishes as he spoke, "Keeping your mother and you all safe is much more important than celebrating my birthday, but I'm thankful that you are doing this for me."

"Aren't you thankful for being alive another year? Mommy says we should be thankful for every new day, and especially our birthdays." She replied earnestly, taking a sip of her orange juice."

Andrea set a plate stacked with pancakes on the table and than divided them between the four plates, "I'm sure Levi is thankful for his birthday, Chloe. Sometimes we forget things when our brains are too busy thinking about more important things."

Levi winked in her direction, "Wow that was very intelligent, Andrea. Where did that come from?"

"I'm not always so dense, you know. I can actually hold a pretty decent conversation all on my own."

"I'm sure," Levi looked at the twins and smiled at them cheekily.

Since Levi only had to be at work in the evening, he decided to take the kids out for the day. He planned to take them to the zoo for the morning and than to their mothers in the afternoon. They all clambered into the Bronco and he drove out to the freeway; the drive to the zoo took over an hour, but it would be worth it.

"I love Saturdays," Andrea exclaimed quietly from her seat beside Levi, "There is no homework to worry about, or school; we can relax and just enjoy the sunshine."

Levi was about to respond to her thoughts, when his cell phone rang, "Dag, this is Levi."

"Levi, we've got the men who were outside your building. They haven't said anything yet, but we found a list of names and phone numbers on Antonio," Sean babbled excitedly into the phone, "Mike is running those numbers as we speak; maybe we'll be able to put this thing behind us, yet."

Mike came on the phone than and gave a report as to how Todd and his crew were doing with the renovations. It seemed that the painting crew had not shown up, so all of Andrea's plans were still with them. Andrea remarked than that she had copies at the apartment and Mike asked them to bring them over later so they could get started.

The morning was spent in total relaxation; Andrea was very helpful feeding the animals with the twins. And after a long train ride around the park, they bought some hotdogs and sat under the shade of some trees to eat.

"Is Mommy ever going to walk again?" Chloe asked, leaning her head up against Levi's shoulder.

Sighing, he kissed the top of her head, "I hope so, sweetie. But we'll just have to see how she does; jah?"

Cole stood up and dusted the crumbs from off his pants, "Can I go play on the swings?"

Levi shook his finger at him, "Aren't you forgetting something?"

He blushed and held his head down, "We have to pray."

"That's right, come, sit down beside me and we'll pray together before you go on the swings."

They sat together and Levi prayed reverently, "Lord, Thank Thee for the food Thou has given us for sustenance in this life. Wilt thou be with us throughout the day and keep us safe from danger. And we pray that Thou will heal those who are sick and wounded both in faith and in body. Cleanse us from every sin and abide within our hearts. Amen."

Long after the children had left his side to play Levi still sat in the shade of the elm thinking about how he could make the pain stop. What could he do to get these men off their backs? Who besides God could help him avenge the wrongdoing of these men? At the beginning of the month, things seemed so normal and at peace; but how could the world seem so different in one day? The only two things that were still the same to him were his love for Abby and the children and his faith in God. To him, nothing in the world seemed more important and he would do everything he could to keep it that way. However, what could he do to end all the pain?

"The Reverend is not in the office today, Levi." Polly Hodgkin's explained, leading him into the small waiting area. As the receptionist of the church, Mrs. Hodgkin's happened to know much about everyone and she didn't hide her knowledge from him, "But if you want to talk to someone else about what has been going on, Terrence Landings is in. He is the new church counselor; he's young but he knows what he's talking about, so maybe he can help."

Levi shuffled his feet uncomfortably; he had never been to a counselor because he never needed to. In his life, he always had someone to talk to and now that he really needed someone's help, it felt a little strange. "I guess that would be alright; I really need someone's point of view on the situation and a little comfort."

Andrea and the twins walked in than and settled in the chairs to wait while he went in, eager to go to their mother afterwards. Once he was assured that they would be fine, he walked with the Polly down the hallway. The door at the end suddenly opened and a tall dark man came out dressed in blue cords and a burgundy button down shirt. He smiled at Polly and than nodded in Levi's direction. "What can I do for you both?"

Before Levi could answer, Polly took hold of his arm and leaned her head on his arm, "This is the gentleman I've been talking about lately. You know, Levi Bontrager, the one with all the trouble in his life?"

Terrence nodded again and held his hand, "Good to meet you sir, you can call me Terrence. Why don't you step in my office, while Polly brings us some coffee?"

"Denki," Levi replied, walking past him into the roomy office.

Pointing to the two black leather sofas, Terrence indicated for him to take a seat and than followed suit by sitting across.

"So, what has brought you to this point, Levi? May I call you Levi?" He took out a file and jotted something down while he spoke.

"Jah, that is okay." Levi settled back in his chair and began to talk. It had been easy for him to explain to himself what had happened; but to someone else it was much harder. "You see," he announced after a while, "I've lived such a plain life before, and now all this craziness has just really gotten to me. I don't know if I'll be able to be strong for Abby or the children any longer. I'm scared every second of every day."

"Have you contacted the police or the press? I know that the press is able to do pretty amazing things these days by broadcasting a crime." He jotted some numbers down on a slip of paper and handed it over, "Teresa Franks is one of the best reporters in Philadelphia as a whole and she happens to be in our particularly quant town as we speak."

Levi took the slip and read the numbers as he spoke, "So, what can she help me with?"

"Well," Terence stood up and walked over to his desk to find a file on the sloppy pile on top of it, "I think she is probably your best option yet; besides prayer that is. She can right certain facts in an article that the normal reader could not apprehend as something important. But, to the trained eye of a specific crime it is very easy to follow the lines."

"Thank you for your time, but I have to get going now. I'm taking the children to see Abby and than I have to meet with Mrs. Franks." Levi stood up and shook the hand Terrence held out before walking back to the waiting area.

Andrea was standing up with a book in her hand, "Are we going now? I really want to see Mom; I miss her."

Grinning widely, Levi nodded and led them out to the Bronco, "I miss her too. Listen, I'm going to drop you off at the home, and than I have some things to do so I'll come back and pick you up later okay?"

"Aww," Chloe whined, "I want you to stay with us, Levi."

Levi helped her up into the truck and secured the seatbelt around her as he spoke, "I know you do, sweetheart, but I need you to spend some time with your Mommy. She needs to have some special time with you."

His heart tugged as he listened to Chloe crying softly in the backseat, and he could tell that everyone was nearing the end of their ropes. Cole was grouchy all the time and despondent and Andrea was completely hiding her feelings altogether. He needed to get things settled so they could live normal lives again.

Levi had a hard time finding the Oracle's newspaper office because it was tucked behind the fire station and Slim Pickin's restaurant. Nevertheless, once inside he was shown immediately to her office and he was surprised at her appearance. He had figured she would be an older woman but instead he found himself being introduced to a woman younger than he found himself. She wore a short suit and her blond hair hung loose around her shoulders; she was definitely not what he expected.

"You're surprised aren't you?" she commented lightly, gesturing for him to take a seat across from her.

Levi blushed and shifted in his seat, "Jah, I thought you would be older."

Teresa laughed and folded her arms on the desk top, "Most people have that reaction when they come and see me; I guess my reputation kind of tricks people."

"I'm sure that is the case, jah." Levi nodded in agreement, immediately liking the spunkiness of the reporter.

"Terence gave me a call a few minutes ago saying that you would be stopping in to talk, but I didn't think you would be here so soon. So, forgive me if I eat my snack while we talk." She took out a zip lock bag filled with carrot sticks and began to munch happily.

"What did he tell you exactly?"

She took a notebook out and read what she had written down, "He told me that you are a witness to a crime and you have had some people after you. Can you tell me everything, from when you overheard these men talking until now? Don't leave anything out, because I can give you all the files I will have for your court case. I presume there will be one, correct?"

For the next hour, Levi explained everything to Teresa as she wrote it all down and asked questions appropriately. Than just as they were finishing up his cell phone rang and it was Sean, who had crucial information for him. He said goodbye to Teresa and thanked her for her help before running outside to talk to his friend.

"So what is this new information you have, Sean?" he leaned his back against the Bronco as he spoke in to the cell, crossing his feet in front of him.

Sean laughed, "No hello for me?"

"Hello Sean, what did you find out?"

"My forensics team found a crate of capsules at Allen's house and there are trace elements of cocaine in the capsules. We need you to come to the bureau office to talk to the narcotics team; can you come?"

"I'll be there right away. This is good news, jah?"

"Jah," Sean copied with a teasing tone, "This is very good news. We're hoping that you can help the forensics team come up with components in the cocaine to match it to someone."

"Don't worry; I'll be there as soon as I can." Levi advised, opening the Bronco's door and lifting himself into the seat, "See you later, Sean."

"Hey, you really are getting better at the English, Levi,"

Levi chuckled, "Well, I learn from the best."

They said goodbye and than Levi concentrated on getting himself to the bureau office in record time.

Chapter Twenty

Abby shifted up in the hospital bed with Andrea's help, and than rested against the pillows supporting her back. Today had started out bad, she had argued with her therapist and her counselor and her lunch had tasted horrible. Now that the kids were around her, she could concentrate on them rather that her own problems. She was coming to terms with the fact that she might never be able to walk again, but the path leading to recovery seemed so long and dark. It was depressing and sometimes she just wanted to lock the door, close the blinds, and sink away from the world. Some days she would just slip off the bed and lay on the cold tiles because it felt safer than the bed. And her head always hurt from the thoughts passing through; she would get strange dreams and visions and her counselor dismissed them too easily. She wished that Levi were near so she could talk to him about them all.

"Mommy, guess what we did this morning?" Cole exclaimed, climbing onto the end of the bed.

Abby pushed her disturbing thoughts away and concentrated on her son's excitement, "I don't know, honey, why don't you tell me?"

"Since it's Levi's birthday today, we made him breakfast and than he took us to the zoo."

Chloe hopped up on the bed beside him and nodded excitedly,

"It was so much fun, Mommy. I love him so much, can he be our Daddy?"

Abby felt the blush creep onto her face and Andrea started to laugh, "I don't know honey, and we have to see what happens in the future. And we don't know what Levi has to say about the matter, do we?"

"No," Chloe hung her head sadly, "But I wish he would be our Daddy, he is so nice."

As the children chatted with each other, Abby took the time to concentrate her thoughts on the love they had for him. She wished and hoped that he still had feelings for her; she wanted to believe that he did but it was very hard.

Meanwhile, at the FBI office, Levi sat in the lab surrounded by agents and lab technicians of every kind. Sean stood at the front of the room ordering people around so they could get started with the briefing.

"Alright everyone lets all take a seat so Dan can begin." Sean advised, gesturing toward the tall bald narcotics investigator standing to the left.

Dan walked to the lectern and pulled it off to the side in order to make the visual of the screen behind him clearer, "Alright, I am sure that you all know why we are here today so I won't go into any more detail than necessary. Some members of my team have found cocaine particles in the capsules that were confiscated from the perpetrator's Lab. Now all we need to do is match these particles to the type of cocaine used by any of our suspects." He than tapped some fingers on the computer screen and a face showed up, "This man, Orlando Sanchez, is well known in our area as a drug distributor but we have never been able to pinpoint any of the drugs on him. We have arrested some of his men on drug smuggling and distribution but never him. If we are able to bring him down, we can get the entire team. I realize that this will take a lot of work to catch this person, but this is the only real evidence we have been able to get so far. It will be worth it for sure."

Levi stood up, "I can run a drug analysis and see what comes up; I'll need some the Lab Techs to help me on this though."

"They're yours," he exclaimed, gesturing for some members of the team to follow Levi.

The team of four followed Levi down the long hallway towards their lab, "What are you studying for, Levi?" a spiky haired member asked curiously.

"Pediatric Surgeon; can I ask what your names are? This will make this much easier."

The crazy haired member held out his hand, "I'm Calvin Smithers, and I have my GED in Forensic Science."

Levi nodded in his direction, "Alright Calvin; why don't you dig up the old records on this Orlando fellow?"

When Calvin left to do as he was asked, the dark haired pony tailed girl came forward, "I'm Hillary Smithers; Calvin's sister, and I have my GED in soil samples and other particles."

"Okay, how about you check over those boxes that were confiscated and see what you can find out to help us."

The last two members followed him into their lab and he found out that the blonde girl was Emily Newman and her friend was Matthew Nielson. They both had GED in substance identification. For the next hour and a half, they spent their time working hard identifying the cocaine substance and trying to find a match.

Suddenly, as Levi was leaning over the microscope he found the same signature on two samples he had been working on. One was from the capsules in the boxes from Larry's lab and the other was an old sample confiscated from one of Orlando's team members. They both had the exact same signature; traces of household elements that could be bought at any general store.

"Matt, I need you to take these results to Sean and Dan. I have a match to the cocaine from Orlando and I think they will really be happy with this," he explained, walking to him and handing him a printout of the results.

"Hey wait a minute!" Calvin exclaimed, "I looked through those old files and found that they used household items to make the cocaine. On the crime scene they found all kinds of items that could be used, so what did you find?"

Levi grinned and gestured for Matt to explain to him their

findings. Just as they were walking out of the room, Hillary came back with a wide smile on her face, "Oh, you are going to like me."

"Really, well what did you find?"

She walked along side of them and handed him a sheet, "At first when I looked at the boxes I couldn't find anything but than I turned them over and on the bottom there was mold forming on the bottom. And when I analyzed it, I found the same components to a sample I had taken from a crime at the old Hunter's Lab at the edge of Flounders Lake. These boxes were first put together there before being transported to Larry's Lab."

Stopping in his tracks, Levi turned to Hillary in surprise, "Are you saying what I think you're saying?"

"Yes," she said with a smile, "We now have the point of origin of Orlando's operation."

Levi was not asked to go along with the SWAT team heading over to the crime sight, so he went over to Abby to visit. When he arrived at the group home and parked the Bronco near the entrance, two men came running up to him excitedly. Clearly one of the men was Mike, with his shorts and marine t-shirt. However, the other happened to be someone that he had not seen in quite a while, Troy.

"Hey buddy, Sean called and told me that they're heading out to find this Orlando fellow," Troy exclaimed, slapping his friend on the back enthusiastically.

"Jah, that is right. We dug around a bit and found some evidence leading to his cartel." He followed the men back into the building as he spoke, "Hopefully this time we found the right man. We are pretty sure, but you never know."

The door to Abby's room stood wide open as the three men walked up, "Well, why don't you visit with Abby for a while, Mike is taking the children back to the apartment. That'll give you some time to yourselves while you wait for the news."

"Denki," he exclaimed to Mike giving him a manly hug, "We need this time together, and it's been so hard to find time for each other."

After the men left with the children, Levi sat beside Abby's bed as she slept and watched her silently. She looked so happy and peaceful;

so different from what she had been like the last time he saw her. Of course, she hadn't shown her uneasiness but he could see the pain in her face. Now, she looked happy and the stress lines on her face had cleared.

While she slept, Levi took a book from the stack beside her bed and began to read. He was entirely engrossed in the novel when he felt a soft hand pat his arm. He looked up to see Abby smiling up at him, "Hey you," she said softly.

"Hey," he place the book back on the stack and took her hand in is, "how are you feeling?"

"Happy....so happy," Abby took her hand and ran it down his cheek gently, "you're here now and I am so happy."

Levi smiled, "Did Mike tell you that Sean is going after Orlando Sanchez the kingpin of drug distribution in this area? He's going to call soon and tell us what they found."

Abby pulled herself up in the bed and than leaned in and kissed him tenderly, and than hugged him tight, "Oh Levi, this is such good news. And now that my memory is completely back I have nothing to worry about anymore."

He pulled her back so he could look in her eyes, "Wait a minute; you got your memory back? When did this happen?"

"Yesterday and this morning; I remember when I first laid eyes on you in the store and fell in love with you. I remember when you comforted me when I needed it and our first kiss. Levi, I remember that I love you more than anything on this earth." Tears formed in her eyes as she spoke, and Levi wiped them away gingerly.

"I love you to, Abby. You are everything to me and I want to spend the rest of my life with you and the kids." He than stood up and sat on the bed in front of her, "Please marry me and make me the happiest man in the world."

Abby started to cry as she pulled him into her embrace, "Of course I will marry you, Levi. You mean the world to me."

Levi started to laugh happily and picked her up into his arms, swinging her around as he kissed her. It seemed like nothing could make him happier than he was at that moment. This was a chance to start over, a new beginning.

Just as he was putting Abby back on the bed, a crowd of people burst into the room and at the front was a smiling Sean, "We did it, Levi. We got them all."

"What?" he exclaimed, jumping up in excitement, "Are you serious?"

Patrick slapped his hand on Sean's shoulder as he spoke, "Yep, we caught them red handed. They had a whole set-up in that place, masked people with gloves preparing the cocaine and crates of capsules already filled. It seems like they had begun the process without the permission of the health board."

"Was Orlando there?"

Sean shook his head, "No, but after a little prodding we got the information from one of the men. I just got news that he is being brought in right now. Larry and Mort and all the other men are all in custody right now, so you have nothing to worry about anymore."

Abby started to cry and she took Levi's hand in hers, "Do you know what this means, honey?"

"Yes, it means we have a chance for a new beginning to our relationship." He bent down to give her a kiss and than said to everyone, "I have asked Abby to marry me and she said yes."

"Well than," Sean said with a grin, "I guess this will make it your engagement present. The FBI has paid in full for a set of prosthetic legs for Abby and all the sessions she needs in physical therapy until she can walk again."

There were many tears and laughter after the news and than Mike came back in the room with the children. Apparently, they had known about the present and had stuck around to be there for the surprise. Everyone than moved to the main hall and the men fired up a barbeque that Mike had in his truck bed. Levi looked at his fiancé with joy, as she hugged Andrea to her. She was so extremely beautiful and she loved him unconditionally, the reality of their engagement still did not sink in. He sighed happily and pulled a chair up beside Abby's wheelchair, she smiled at him and clasped his hand in hers. Now they had started their relationship over and were eager to start with a new beginning.

Epilogue
(One year later)

Abby stared across the back lawn of her newly finished home and watched as Cole jumped high to catch the baseball thrown his way. So much had happened since the day Levi had proposed to her in that hospital room. She looked down had her extended tummy and smiled happily to herself, the doctors had not believed it possible but she had proved them wrong. Also, she had proved them wrong about the use of her new legs. Of course, it took a long time to get used to them, she still couldn't use them all the time, but they had helped her walk down the aisle, and she treasured them for that.

"Honey, I'm going in for some iced tea, would you like me to bring you some?" Levi asked, suddenly breaking her from her thoughts.

"That'd be great, thanks darling."

He bent down, kissed her gently, and put his hand on her belly, "I am so lucky to have you as my wife. I love you."

"I love you to." Abby watched than as he strode through the porch screen door leading to the kitchen. He was such an amazing man and every day she fell further in love with him. Levi worked hard at the clinic five days a week and spent every other waking moment with the family. Already he had started building baby furniture, while she looked through catalogues for new accessories for the baby room.

Levi was just pushing his way out the door when Andrea came

running up behind him and nearly pushed him over, "Hey girl, watch were you're going! You nearly made me spill the juice."

"Sorry Dad, I just have some great news. Can you get everyone together for me on the back porch? I'm just going to wait for Walter to arrive before I say anything."

Levi nodded in her direction and watched her bound off to wait for her boyfriend to arrive; clearly, she had some great news to tell.

A few minutes later, the entire family sat on the back porch with Chloe sitting on her father's lap and Walter and Andrea sitting side by side on the swing.

Abby grinned at them, "So, what is the great news you wanted us to hear?"

"We're getting married!" Walter exclaimed pertly, swinging his arm around his girl's shoulder.

While Abby and Levi gasped, Andrea jabbed Walter in the side, "Very funny, don't give them a heart attack now." She looked at her parents and rolled her eyes, "You don't have to worry we won't be getting married yet if I have any say in the matter."

"Gut," Levi exclaimed as he sighed deeply, "Now tell us the real news before we all get panicky."

"Remember the scholarship I applied for at the Art School in Landsville?" she giggled as she spoke, "I got it, Mom. I'm going to the art college for free, can you believe it?"

Everyone started to laugh and cry at the same time, and took turns hugging the excited Andrea. It took a very long time before everyone settled down and Abby sat down beside her husband and took his hand in his.

"Levi, we certainly have much to be thankful for, don't we?"

He nodded and put an arm around her shoulder, "Jah, we do darling, we definitely do."

Background information:

I was born in Chilliwack, BC, into a large Dutch family being the eleventh sibling out of twelve. Growing up in the small town of Rosedale, I always had an amazing imagination in both play and talk and I would come up with the wildest stories. From a young age, I knew that I wanted to become a writer and I practiced constantly. I took writing courses at College later and other correspondence classes. All these lessons prepared me for my dream, to publish my first book. While writing this book, I got to know the characters very well and soon they felt like real people in my life. It was very easy to depict them in the story than, because I could see them right in front of me as I wrote. I hope that as you have read this book, you were able to picture them as clearly as I have.